ADA   Adams, Harold,
        1923-

Sus pense

        A perfectly proper
        murder.

$18.95

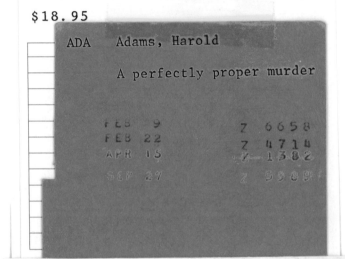

ADA   Adams, Harold

A perfectly proper murder

FEB 9   Z 6658
FEB 22   Z 4718
APR 15   Z 1382
SEP 27   Z 5989

A Perfectly Proper Murder

Also by Harold Adams

The Man Who Was Taller Than God

A Carl Wilcox Mystery

A Perfectly Proper Murder

Harold Adams

Walker and Company
New York

To Will Jones, friend,
host, and critic par excellence.

First published in the United States of America in 1993
by Walker Publishing Company, Inc.

Published simultaneously in Canada by Thomas Allen & Son
Canada, Limited, Markham, Ontario

Library of Congress Cataloging-in-Publication Data
Adams, Harold, 1923–
A perfectly proper murder: a Carl Wilcox mystery / Harold Adams.
p.   cm.
ISBN 0-8027-3237-2
1. Detectives—South Dakota—Fiction. I. Title.
PS3551.D367P46   1993
813'.54—dc20   93-14721
CIP

Printed in the United States of America
2 4 6 8 10 9 7 5 3 1

A Perfectly Proper Murder

▽

1

I WAS BORN and raised in Corden, a town of 1,351 people, and have always been most comfortable in places that size. There are thirty-two burgs between one thousand and two thousand in the state, so I figured if I worked steady and moved often, I could paint signs in every one of them before winter.

That's how I came to be in Podunkville when Basil Ecke got smacked in the kisser with a metal rod that caught him under the nose and on the rise, knocking that little bone up into his brain like a dart and killing him quick as an icepick in the ear.

I reached town late Tuesday afternoon during one of the two downpours allotted that summer, parked in front of a café with a sign that needed retouching, pelted inside, and had my choice of any seat at the counter. A lonely round waitress greeted me with a look that suggested she didn't think I could pay for a meal.

I ordered the pork roast dinner and asked who in town offered room and board reasonable. She said she'd check with the boss, and a few minutes later, before I got my grub, a squat character in dark gray pants and a white shirt came around, said his name was Jim Leslie and what did I do.

"Signs," I said. "Big and small, plain and fancy. All first-class."

"Yah? Ever know a fella named Larry?"

"You bet. Taught me the business."

He brightened. "No kidding? What happened to him?"

"Died. Lungs went."

He sat down heavily beside me and leaned his elbows on the counter. His wide mouth drooped, and he blinked so hard I thought he was going to cry.

"That's awful. Had family, didn't he?"

"Wife, two boys, and a girl."

"How they doing?"

"Mother works at the county courthouse, girl takes care of the house, does the cooking. Older boy works at the bakery, youngest runs the popcorn machine at the show-house and cleans up the place every day. They make out."

He wagged his gray head slowly. "Funny. First times Larry came around I took him for a gypsy. Had an old Model T and slept in a tent by it. Never gave him any business till about his third year through, but after that he always stopped in. Real nice fella. Smart. Did the sign out front."

"I noticed. Must've been a while back."

He blinked at me. "You got family?"

I shook my head. "Married once. It didn't take."

He asked my name and showed no reaction when I told him, which was a relief. It doesn't usually help me if people recognize it.

"Tell you what," he said as his waitress delivered my meal, "when you finish here, go south on First, and in the middle of the second block, on your left, you'll see a brown house with a closed-in front porch. That's the Widow Bower's place. She rents rooms reasonable, keeps a clean house, and sets a decent table. Heavy on vegetables and light on meat, but you don't like it come back here for suppers and she won't be much put out."

I thanked him, he went back to his kitchen, and I worked on the meal, which was no chore at all. Afterward I paid my quarter, and a few minutes later parked my heap in front of the brown house.

Unhappily the Widow Bower was about thirty years past what I'd hoped for, and it was plain when she answered my knock and looked me over that I wasn't exactly the answer to her prayers, either. I told her Jim Leslie had sent me, and that warmed her about half a degree. She took me up to see the room.

It was probably bigger than my cubbyhole at the Wilcox Hotel, but the whopping bed with its oak head and footboards shrank it to the size of a closet. A matching bureau was squeezed against the east wall, crowding the single window, and an oversized dressing table had been shoehorned into the space along the west side. All this was topped with a white washbowl and matching pitcher with soap in a dish on the right and a towel rack on the left. I had to walk sideways to get between the furniture and the bed. A braided rug in shades of gray and maroon covered the floor almost wall to wall. If you wanted to sit down in the room, you could take any part of the bed you chose.

The bathroom, half again as big, was down the hall about a dozen paces.

For this and board she wanted fifty cents a day.

I agreed, figuring if the food wouldn't do I'd move out after the first night. She asked for a dollar in advance. That made me think a couple seconds, but finally I handed it over and the bargain was set. For the first time, Widow Bower dredged up a smile.

When I went out to carry in my bag, a big dude in a navy blue suit gave me the evil eye from the porch of a neighboring house set well back on a double lot. The size and corner location made it obvious he was a hotshot, and the fancy duds let you know he took himself seriously. I could imagine how delighted he was to see my type contaminating his territory.

Being a natural-born diplomat, I wished him good evening in a tone an innocent man would take for friendly.

"There's room around back," he told me, "where you can park that tin lizzie."

This guy was anything but innocent. His voice was hacksaw gentle, his beetle brows over fierce brown eyes tried to bully me, and it all brought out my sweet side.

"Well, thanks a lot, but I figure it's safer out front where

I can keep an eye on it. This looks like a neighborhood could give me problems."

He glared a second, then stomped down the walk to his gleaming Packard, got in, and slammed the door.

Back in the house, the Widow Bower asked who I'd spoken to, and I told her the bogeyman next door.

"Mr. Ecke spoke to you?" she asked with raised eyebrows.

"Yup. You good friends?"

"Like cat and dog. What'd he say?"

I told her. And what I'd answered.

"Oh my," she said with a malicious grin, "he's not used to that."

"What is he?"

"Well, among other things, he owns the drugstore. He's an alderman—likes to think he runs the town—and actually does, to some extent. You really won't gain anything being smart with him."

I admitted I made lots of mistakes like that and went up to try out the bed.

It was just dandy. I slept right through Ecke's murder.

▽

2

WHEN I CAME down for breakfast it was almost nine, and the Widow Bower was pouring coffee for an overweight gent with shaggy eyebrows, big ears, and a matching nose sprouting hair long enough to make it look like he was beginning a mustache.

"This is Mr. Wilcox," the widow announced. "Meet Officer Hurlbut."

Officer Hurlbut considered me with disapproval.

"I hear you're a sign painter," he said.

"Is that illegal?" I asked, sitting down on the chair to his left.

He swigged coffee, lowered the cup with a quiet click on the saucer, and peered at me through his brows.

"You talked with Mr. Ecke last night."

"Yup. He suggested I park my car out back. I said I'd rather leave it out front. What're you getting at?"

"We'll work around to that." He hauled a goosenecked pipe from his right coat pocket, took a tobacco pouch from the left one, and started loading up.

"What happened right after you talked with Mr. Ecke?" he asked.

"He got in his Packard and drove off. I came inside, told Mrs. Bower what happened, and went to bed."

"You didn't maybe get up and go out to check on your car in the night?" he asked, tamping the tobacco down.

"No."

"Just slept the sleep of the innocent, eh?"

"That's right. What's happened to Ecke?"

"What'd you guess?"

"Wherever he went in his Packard, somebody smacked him. Or maybe he had an accident?"

He took some time lighting the pipe and smoking up the room.

"You're close. Somebody killed him. Dead. Seems to me I've heard of Carl Wilcox before. An ex-con, a fighting man. That's you, right?"

"You want to know about me, call Joey Paxton, in Corden, he's the town cop and knows me. I've even subbed for him. Or call Lieutenant Baker, in Aquatown."

"Uh-huh. Getting back to last night. You claim you never left the house after you went up to your room about nine?"

"Ask Mrs. Bower."

"I did. But she admits she's a heavy sleeper. Might not've heard."

She asked me how I'd like my eggs. I said straight up, and she delivered a few minutes later with bacon, toast, and coffee.

Officer Hurlbut watched me eat. After about half a dozen puffs the pipe went out. I guessed he was trying to decide whether a killer might have a good appetite or not. He saw I had no problem putting away groceries.

The widow offered us both cinnamon rolls when I thought I was through, and we both accepted.

"Who else have you talked to this morning?" I asked.

"You're the first. I heard about the killing around four this morning. Didn't have any suspects. Got talking with Jim Leslie at breakfast, and he mentioned this fella who'd known Larry, the sign painter. He never heard of you, but I had, and it seemed worth checking out since you were staying next door and Mr. Ecke didn't have any enemies. You mind emptying your pockets on the table here?"

I did but didn't see any percentage in refusing and put it all out. A wallet with twelve bucks in it, seventy-eight cents in change, my jackknife, cigarette bag, package of papers, and matches. He tucked away the pipe and pawed my stuff over as if he expected to find something telling and finally concluded I traveled light. Then he got up and said he was going to look over my room.

"Be my guest," I said and kept him company so he couldn't plant anything.

He didn't enjoy it and had a hell of a time working his bulk between the bed and the bureau, but he did a more creditable job than I'd have expected. He came up with sniffles.

"Okay," he said as we went downstairs, "I had to check."

"Was Ecke robbed?"

"No."

"What were you looking for?"

"Anything. But mostly a murder weapon."

"How was he killed?"

"Doc Penzler's doing an autopsy—he'll tell me when he feels like it."

"Where was he found?"

He gave me a sly look. "By your car. Out in back. It's up on blocks and your wheels are all off."

3

IT WAS THE biggest surprise since Ollie Banks broke my
nose with a rock from his slingshot when I was sitting on
the peak of our barn celebrating my eighth birthday.

I stood by the car under an apple tree and gawked at my
Model T perched on four concrete blocks.

"I can't picture the dude I saw last night moving the
flivver, let alone taking off the tires," I said to Officer Hurlbut, who stood beside me nodding.

"He didn't do it," said the law. "I'd bet my wife on it."

Not knowing what he thought she was worth, I couldn't
figure how positive that made him.

"So who would? And why?"

"One of his boys, maybe. Overheard you giving the old
man lip, decided to put you in your place."

"You talked to them already?"

He sighed. "I'll have to."

"Can I come along?"

He considered that and said first he better call Corden and
Aquatown.

He didn't invite me along, so I started putting the wheels
back on the flivver. I'd only done two when he came back.

"All right," he said, "let's go."

Evidently Joey and the lieutenant had been convincing.
We headed for the Ecke mansion.

Evadne Ecke was another surprise, only this was a good
one. No more than thirty, red-haired, slim, and solemn, she
might have been Ecke's daughter. Her expression was more

thoughtful than bereaved, and I saw a fading bruise on her left cheek. When Hurlbut asked to see the boys, she told him they were up in their rooms.

Hurlbut frowned. "They know what's happened?"

"They know their father's dead." Her voice was low but distinct.

"This's Carl Wilcox," Hurlbut said, jerking his thumb at me. "He's worked on murders in Corden and Aquatown."

She considered me without noticeable enthusiasm and nodded.

"How old are the boys?" I asked.

"Terrell's seventeen, Baxter's fifteen."

"They're not yours?"

Hurlbut's head jerked as he turned to give me a disapproving scowl, but she only nodded. "I was Basil's second wife. His first died in an accident."

"What kind?"

"She fell down the stairs."

Hurlbut, looking nervous and crowded, asked if she'd call the boys down.

She went up after them. Hurlbut stood awkwardly, fumbled with the pipe in his pocket, finally abandoned it, and looked wistfully toward the living room and its couch and easy chairs. While he obviously felt the need to rest his feet, he only shuffled a little and kept standing.

"Notice the bruise on her cheek?" I asked.

He nodded impatiently.

"Did Ecke slap her around?"

He hitched up his pants, scowled, and reminded me the man was fresh dead.

"When'd the first wife die?"

"Eight years, more or less."

"She ever have any bruises?"

"Not that I know of. What're you trying to get at?"

"I was wondering about you saying the dude had no enemies."

"A man can straighten his wife out and not make enemies.

Women like to know who's boss."

"Yeah," I said, "some of 'em are dying to. How long's he been married to this one?"

"About seven years."

Evadne came back and said the boys would be down in a moment—would we like coffee?

Hurlbut beamed yes and happily parked his hefty carcass in an easy chair as she went into the kitchen. She returned with a tray as the boys appeared, both in clean slacks and pressed shirts. Their shoes weren't shined, but they weren't dusty either.

Hurlbut began with an apology for bothering them but explained we had to get facts straight quick as possible. The older boy, Terrell, watched him sullenly and avoided looking my way. Baxter looked a good four years younger than his brother and kept sneaking peeks at me. Both had blue eyes, but Terrell's were cold. Baxter's seemed vulnerable. Terrell had the build of a football lineman with a jaw to match. Baxter looked thin and fragile. I got the feeling his big brother always crowded him away from the trough at mealtime.

"I got to know," said Hurlbut, "did you boys hear your father talking with Mr. Wilcox here last night?"

Baxter looked at his brother, who said no with more belligerence than seemed natural.

"Did your dad maybe call you from somewheres else and tell you to move the Model T next door and take the wheels off?"

"Why'd he do that?" demanded Terrell. His tone let Hurlbut know he thought he was an idiot.

"Somebody moved the car. It ain't likely your dad did or anybody else heard them talking, so I got to find out."

That brought nothing, and he asked Evadne if she'd heard us.

"I heard Basil's voice but don't know what he said."

"Where were you at the time?"

"Right here."

Ecke had been standing on the porch just outside this room.

"What were you doing?" I asked.

She gave me a brown-eyed stare. "Knitting."

I asked if she knew where her husband was going when he left. She said he'd not told her and she didn't ask.

Hurlbut asked Baxter if he'd heard anything and got a head shake. After a few more questions he thanked them, hauled himself out of the chair, thanked Evadne, and headed out.

When we were on the front walk, I suggested we tour the grounds. He looked surprised but agreed.

The double lot covered the block's end and had a slight rise to where the house stood. Large elms spread their branches along the south side, and a hedge bordered the sidewalk on the north.

"No neighbors close enough to hear us last night," I said.

Hurlbut agreed but said Ecke could've called back when he got where he was going.

"Where?"

"Maybe his brother's farm. It's five miles west. We'll run out there."

I began wondering why he was accepting my involvement but got into his car without worrying about it.

Homer Ecke's place was a little better than the average farm in South Dakota those days. The housepaint wasn't peeling and the back stoop didn't sag, but the front door stood two feet above the bare earth and had been covered with tar paper nailed on with laths. Like most farms in our territory, people used only the back door, which led out to where all the work was. The front room was called the parlor and was used only for weddings, funerals, and maybe an occasional anniversary party.

We parked on a bare patch of ground near the house. A stout woman watched from behind the screen door as we approached.

"That's Mae," Hurlbut muttered, "with an *e*."

It was plain he despised her, but he managed to speak in a civil tone as we stopped by the stoop.

"You heard the news?" he asked.

"What news?"

"It's bad. Where's Homer?"

"Out in the barn. What's on your mind or whatever it is you got between your ears?"

Her voice had the hard edge of disapproving authority I always heard from my old man. If anything, it was even nastier.

"Basil Ecke's dead. Murdered."

Her mouth tightened a second, then twisted.

"One of his women's husbands finally got him, eh?"

"Did he come out here last night?"

"No."

"He left his house and drove somewheres last night a little past eight. I thought he might've visited Homer."

"Think again, if it's not too much of a strain."

"I got to talk with Homer."

"So go to the barn, whatever good it'll do you. He's drunk. Facing his problems like a man."

We walked toward the barn. I glanced back and saw her mean eyes watching steadily.

It was tempting to needle Hurlbut about his claim that Ecke had no enemies, but the set of his mouth decided me against it.

$\triangledown$

4

Homer wasn't in sight when we entered the barn, but after Hurlbut called we heard movement in the loft, looked up, and saw a bleary face staring down. It disappeared, and then two feet under a broad fanny came in sight as he backed down the ladder. He turned slowly, took an unsteady step, and leaned against the wall.

We walked up to him. He wore bib overalls, high shoes, and a blue denim shirt with the sleeves rolled up. I could smell the booze a yard away.

"Wanna drink?" he asked.

"I got bad news," said Hurlbut.

"You gonna arrest me?"

"It's about your brother, Basil."

Homer blinked stupidly, looked at the straw-covered floor, and sighed.

"He was murdered last night," said Hurlbut.

"Ah!" Homer tipped his head back and bumped it against the wall.

"Did he come out here last night?"

The tired eyes widened slightly and tried to focus on the lawman's face.

"Why'd he come here? He ain't been in eight years."

"He went off somewheres last night. I don't think it could've been far from home, because he wound up in his own yard."

Homer's face had about as much shape as a balloon that's lost air and started crinkling up. His mouth sagged, and his graying hair was tousled and hadn't been cut in months. He took a deep breath, let it out, suggested we all sit down, and sagged to the floor.

"How long you been drinking, Homer?" asked Hurlbut.

A look of cunning came into the bleary eyes. "Never quit."

"Homer, don't gimme that. You like a drink but you don't live on it. Why's Mae even ornerier than usual?"

"She's down on men," he said. "Hates 'em all. Me included."

"She was great friends with Basil's first wife, right?"

"Olivia—oh yah. Went to school together."

"Mae was mad he got married again so quick, wasn't she?"

The bleary eyes rose to meet the lawman's gaze, and the sagging mouth drew up into a vague grin.

"That was some of it, yah."

"What else?"

"You know damn well, she never kept it no secret."

Hurlbut scowled at the floor.

"She thought Basil knocked his wife down those stairs, didn't she?" I asked.

Homer's eyes turned to me. He blinked and turned to Hurlbut. "Who's he?"

Hurlbut told him. It registered nothing. Homer gave me a bleary stare.

"Why's he with you?" he asked Hurlbut without taking his eyes from me.

"Lieutenant Baker, in Aquatown, and Joey, in Corden, said he could solve murders."

I repeated my question.

"It don't mean nothing," he said. "She's always shot off her mouth every chance. She don't believe nothing bad ever happened without it was a man's fault. If a woman bites her tongue or gets the flu, some man's gotta take the blame."

"Nobody pays any attention to her," Hurlbut told me.

"You got any notion where your brother might've been going last night?" I asked.

"Not the foggiest."

We left him still sitting on the floor, staring into space, and as we approached Hurlbut's Model A, Mae stepped out on her back porch. She was built like a gunnysack of potatoes with a leather belt cinching the middle.

"Look for one of the husbands he cuckolded," she yelled. "It might take a year, but you'll find it was one of them if you look hard enough."

Hurlbut nodded in her direction, climbed heavily into the car, and started the engine. I settled beside him. Mae stayed on the step, glaring after us.

"I guess Ecke was a chaser," I said.

He scowled. "There's talk, yeah."

I tried to get more, but he was busy brooding and didn't answer. Finally I asked if Ecke had any daughters. He said yes, Jennifer and Pauline. "Jen's eighteen, Pauline's twelve."

"Where were they when we were at the house?"

"Upstairs, most likely."

"We ought to talk to them."

"They won't know nothing."

He drove back to Ecke's house, parked in front, and twisted on the seat to face me.

"All right," he said, "I'm gonna leave you ask the questions, okay?"

I said fine, lead on.

The younger girl, Pauline, answered his knock. She was blond, blue-eyed, fair, and slim as a weasel. She examined me from my scuffy shoes to my unorganized crown and invited us into the living room, where we found her stepmother and the older sister knitting on the couch.

Jennifer was sleek and long-legged with short brown hair, blue eyes, a narrow nose, thin lips, and trim ankles. She examined me with critical eyes and no expression.

"What'd Homer say?" asked Evadne.

"Basil didn't go out there," said Hurlbut.

"He said Basil hadn't been out there for eight years," I said. "Why wouldn't he visit his brother in that long?"

"Maybe he didn't like farms," said Jennifer. Her voice was soft as a kitten's fur.

"It sounds more like he didn't care for his brother."

The two women returned my stare without expression, but Pauline spoke up.

"It was Aunt Mae."

Jennifer gave her little sister a tolerant smile that showed deep dimples.

"What do you mean?" I asked.

"She blamed Daddy for Mama's fall."

"Why?"

Pauline suddenly turned shy and looked toward Jennifer.

"Aunt Mae doesn't like any men," said the sister. "She and Daddy never got along."

"She liked your mother fine, though, didn't she?"

Jennifer blushed and finally nodded. "Yes. She loved Mama."

"Your father ever hit your mother?"

"No," she said firmly, meeting my stare dead-on.

I heard a small sound from Pauline and looked at her.

"Did you see him hit your mother?"

"Come on," said Jennifer in a voice not so soft, "she was only four when Mama died."

The sisters stared at each other briefly, then Pauline looked at me and shook her head.

I turned to the widow.

"Where'd you get the bruise on your cheek?"

"It was an accident. I bumped into an open cabinet door."

All this had upset Hurlbut, and before I could ask anything more, he thanked the women and said we had to be getting along.

We drove two blocks downtown and went over to the doctor's office to check progress.

Doc Penzler was a brisk man not quite my size, with a trim gray beard, bright blue eyes, a good crop of gray hair, and a firm, red-lipped mouth. He shook hands with me, said he knew Doc Feeney in Corden and had heard about me from him.

"Nothing good, I'd guess."

"Quite the contrary. He thinks you're a remarkable specimen with an incredible constitution and recuperative powers. He's convinced that pound for pound you're as fit as any man he's ever examined, despite the bowlegs and regrettable tendencies toward overindulgence and excess."

"What'd you find killed our man last night?"

"Remarkable case," he said with satisfaction. "It's likely the assailant used a metal rod, roughly the circumference of your little finger. It struck on the upswing above the mouth, at the front of the septum, smashed the bone there, and drove it like a dart directly into the brain, causing a massive hemorrhage and killing him instanter. It was either an extremely fortuitous or a remarkably skillful blow by a practiced hand. Most likely done with a poker or something similar."

"How about the edge of a hand?"

"You mean one of those oriental blows? I think not. The skin is lacerated, and I'm reasonably certain it was caused by something metallic."

Hurlbut and I walked back to his car and stood under the hot sun, staring at the few cards parked diagonally along First Avenue catching dust blown from the graveled street by a steady wind.

"A poker," he muttered. "Now we got to go looking for pokers?"

"Maybe a big screwdriver, or a piece of reinforcing rod."

"I haven't seen anything like that around here."

"You probably haven't been looking. What we need's a peek inside the house where our man was last. Only we don't know where the hell that was."

▽

5

I ASKED HURLBUT if Ecke's Drugstore had an employee who knew something about the boss. He said Alex Solomon, the pharmacist, probably knew him as well as anybody.

We were greeted by a stocky young woman with a pug nose, inquiring eyes, and a no-nonsense attitude. She greeted Officer Hurlbut with a glance and gave me the once-over as if she thought I might be handcuffed to him. My grin brought no response. Hurlbut told me this was Elaine Fitzgerald and headed for the pharmacist in back. I followed a step before glancing back quick and catching her half-smile.

Alex was built on the same lines as the clerk, only he bulged where she tapered. He peered at us through glasses that magnified his eyes owlishly and gave me the feeling he could see into my head. His wrinkled white coat looked washer worn and needed another soaking.

"No," he told us before Hurlbut spoke, "I didn't kill him and I don't know who did."

"I wasn't going to ask that. What I want to know is, you any idea where he might've been going in his car last night around nine?"

Alex tilted his head back. "How the hell'd I know that?"

"You knew him better than most. What kind of business would he have at night?"

"Monkey business. What else?"

"You telling me he had a girlfriend?"

"You telling me you hadn't heard?"

They glowered at each other, and finally Hurlbut jerked

his head my way and gave my name and why I was along.

"Yeah," said Alex, giving me his magnified stare, "I heard about him. The boozing cowboy con turned cop. He looks sober so far."

"Who was Ecke messing with?"

"You really don't know?"

"I'm asking you."

"Well, I know of one at least. Heard of others. I can't believe you're blind and deaf."

Hurlbut took a deep breath and looked around the store. High shelves made tunnels, so he couldn't see much.

"Where's Polly?"

"Went home sick when she heard about the boss."

"You're telling me he was fooling around with Polly, right?"

"Did I say that?" He looked at me. "Did you hear me say anything like that?"

"I picked up a hint. Didn't like your boss a lot, did you?"

"I didn't not like him enough to kill him, I'll tell you that. You might say I was shy of respect. He knew it when he was alive, and I'm not hypocrite enough to pretend otherwise now he's dead. Did you really kill a man in Toqueville?"

"We didn't come here to talk about me. Where were you last night at nine?"

"At home. With my very own wife and my own kid. And I didn't slip out and slay my boss and run home to kiss my wife. Old Sherlock here'll give you my address you want to go talk with my wife. The kid won't tell you anything—he's only two and a little slow yet. At talking, I mean. He's not slow any other way we've noticed."

"Is Polly married?" I asked Hurlbut.

He nodded.

I looked at Alex. "Where'd Ecke meet Polly away from here?"

"I've not said she was the one I knew about. But if she was, I'd guess they met different places to try and keep from being noticed."

"Anybody ever tell you they saw them meeting some-place?"

"I didn't say that. You guys keep making things up."

I watched him in silence for a moment, and he didn't like it. He didn't quite squirm, but I caught a twitch.

"Was he fooling with the other girl, Elaine?"

He thought that was funny. He laughed and shook his head. I hoped she hadn't overheard my question or caught his reaction.

We went over to Polly's house. It was on the north side of town, very small and set back on a sloping lot of rare grass, lush dandelions, and stubby weeds.

It took a while before Polly answered Hurlbut's knock. She'd plainly been crying and didn't want to let us in, but Hurlbut firmly opened the door and moved past her into the living room, which was deep in shadows caused by closed shades.

He didn't introduce me. She kept taking nervous glances my way but was too intimidated to raise questions. For a moment the three of us sat in silence.

"You were messing around with the boss, right?" said Hurlbut.

She lifted her head and met his stare.

"I loved him," she said huskily.

It was hard to tell in the poor light, but I guessed when she hadn't been crying she might be a good-looking woman. She was a little taller than average, built on lean lines, and had fine, light brown hair only long enough to hide her ears. The mouth was wide, thin, and drooped like a tragic mask.

"Does your husband know?"

She stared at the floor. "Everybody knows."

"He try to stop it?"

She shook her head, then lifted her gaze and took me in.

"He didn't do anything. He thought if he did I might lose my job. That's all that matters to him."

I tried to look as surprised and shocked as she wanted, but she wasn't quite satisfied with my effort and looked to see Hurlbut's. He came through fine.

"How long's it been going on?" I asked.

"A year."

"How long've you been working for him?"

"Nearly two and a half years. We were mutually attracted from the start but didn't do anything about it for a long time. Finally we couldn't help ourselves."

"What'd your husband say?"

"He said when Basil got tired of me I'd lose my job."

"You believe that?"

"He never got tired of me." There was both pride and defiance in that. She looked a little better to me.

"You meet him last night?" asked Hurlbut.

"No."

That stopped both of us for a moment. Finally I asked if she could prove it. She said no. She was home alone. Her husband had been at the pool hall until late and came home drunk.

"You know anybody else he might've gone to visit at nine at night?"

"No."

She said that with a hopelessness that hinted to me she had some ideas.

"Alex said the boss had more than one other woman," I told her. "Is he right?"

She lowered her gaze to the clenched hands in her lap and whispered, "I don't know for sure."

"Any idea of who?"

She shook her head.

"Don't you want the killer caught?" demanded Hurlbut.

"It won't matter to Basil," she said.

"It could matter to the family," I said. "There'll always be talk if the real killer's not nailed. He beat his wife, didn't he?"

"I don't know anything about that. We didn't talk about his family."

"What did he talk about?"

She shrugged. "It doesn't matter now."

And that's all we could get out of her.

6

At supper the Widow Bower's two other boarders showed up: Billie Fielding and Jack Springer. Billie was a gaunt old woman with a turkey neck, a hawk's beak, and attacking eyes. She hated me on sight but gradually turned only hostile and ended up civic when I listened to her talk and asked questions that moved her on.

She allowed she knew cousins of mine who farmed near Hazel, about twenty miles southeast of Corden.

"Hal Wilcox is a respectable man," she told me in a tone that advised me to follow his example, "He did well back when we got rain. Probably scratching now. Lost his wife early. The children helped out and he finally married again. . . ."

Jack was a young man, doing work connected with the WPA—I never understood what. He kidded the two old ladies, praised the widow's cooking, and marveled at Billie's memory, probing it regularly. The widow doted on him and Billie accepted him.

They avoided talk about the murder until we were almost through with banana cream pie. Then Billie nailed me with her dark eyes and demanded to know how the investigation was going.

I said it hadn't gone far.

"He was one of those men born to be murdered," she said. "It was always plain—but now it's happened everybody pretends shock. They say, 'How could it happen, who in the world would do such a thing?' and nobody admits half the town would love to've done it."

"Why's that?"

"Because they're hypocrites, that's why."

"I didn't mean why'd they say it—I mean why'd so many hate him?"

"Because he was a brute and a bully, that's why. Murdered his first wife—nobody can tell me different. He mayn't intended to, but the way he treated her I don't doubt he hit her and she fell down the stairs. She stayed in the house half the time to hide her bruises. He's hit the new wife too—only she won't hide it—she doesn't mind if people know. Wants 'em to is more like it."

We all thought that over while Billie glared at us accusingly. When no one spoke, she gave her head a jerk.

"There's still worse," she said with satisfaction.

"Worse than murder?" asked the Widow Bower.

Billie nodded positively.

"Adultery?" asked the widow.

"Incest!" announced Billie.

"Oh really," said the widow, "that's going rather far—"

"He went as far as a man can go—and now he's in perdition for it!"

After supper I helped the widow carry dishes out to the kitchen when the other boarders left the dining room.

"You mustn't take Billie too seriously," she told me.

"Oh?"

"She's very bitter about Mr. Ecke. After a year ago he accused her of shoplifting in his store. I don't think it was intentional—you can tell she has a great memory and considerable imagination, but she's terribly absentminded at times. According to her, she picked up toothpaste she intended to buy and on the way to the counter got distracted by something else and put it in her bag so she'd have both hands free and then when she left forgot about it. But Mr. Ecke'd been watching her—he watched everybody, I can tell you, and he stopped her. He didn't prosecute, but he didn't keep what happened a secret, and she's hated him ever since."

"So you don't think Ecke beat his wives or chased women?"

"Well, he had a violent temper, and I'm sure Evadne was often saucy and know that Olivia, his first wife, could be very provoking. As for woman chasing, the fact is a great number of women are attracted by successful and bossy men, and Basil had a weakness for pretty faces. I'm afraid he encouraged them, in fact. But incest? No. I'll never believe that."

I went around to City Hall and found Officer Hurlbut drinking coffee and puffing on his goosenecked pipe. He listened glumly to my report on discussions of the murder victim at the Widow Bower's.

"You listen to old women," he told me, "and you're liable to hear most anything."

"Has the older Ecke girl got a boyfriend?" I asked.

"Jennifer? I suppose so—why?"

"Just wondering. How do the Ecke kids get on with each other?"

"Like most kids, I guess. Fight some, play some. What you getting at?"

"Just trying to get the picture."

He was too town-proud to be any help, so after a while I said I'd see him later. If my leaving broke his heart, he hid it well.

Polly Astor still hadn't come back to work when I dropped in at the drugstore. Elaine was friendly. I liked her being short and solid and admired her tapered waist, trim ankles, and pretty hands. I asked if she knew the Ecke kids at all.

"Sure. Why?"

"How'd they get along with their old man?"

She stared at me soberly with her gray eyes, and I thought she was going to ask what business I had snooping. Then she pursed her lips and shrugged.

"Can't say I know. Except for Terrell. He can't get along with anybody but Jennifer. Baxter was afraid of his father, but then, he's afraid of everyone. Pauline likes everybody.

From what I've seen, which isn't that much, Jenny was respectful and sort of mother-henned the other kids."

"How'd they get on with their stepmother?"

"I don't know. I never saw them out together."

She was silent a moment, and I let her think.

"Ever hear any talk one way or the other?" I asked.

She gave me her direct look again.

"You think Terrell might've killed his father, don't you?"

"He wouldn't be the first kid to kill his old man. It's something we have to check out."

"We," she said. "What are you, some kind of deputy?"

A thin-skinned man would have been embarrassed. I waved my hand.

"Officer Hurlbut asked me to help. Since I started out as his favorite suspect, I naturally figure it's smart to go along. I'm not poking into the town's business just because I'm nosy."

"Okay," she granted, "I can see sense in that."

"You know anybody besides Polly that Ecke was messing with?"

She gave me a sharp look.

"I didn't say I knew Polly was messing with him."

"You work here, you're smart. Don't try to kid me you didn't notice anything. Polly's already admitted to Hurlbut and me she and Ecke were into it, so you're not going to be ratting on her."

"She told you two that?"

I nodded.

She stayed skeptical a moment before she evidently decided the affair was too well known around town for Polly to pretend it wasn't common knowledge.

"Poor Polly," she said.

"She told us even her husband knew—and didn't fight it because he didn't want her fired."

"That sounds like him." Her disgust was obvious.

"What's he like?"

"Shiftless bum."

"Where's he work?"

"He takes odd jobs now and again when he feels up to it. Sweeps out the dance hall, helps at the lumberyard when they're shorthanded. That kinda thing."

"How'd Polly happen to marry him?"

"When they met he was a violinist, and everybody thought he'd be famous one day. They married just before he went to work for the Minneapolis Symphony. After about a year and a half something happened. Some say he started drinking and got fired. Anyway, he and Polly came back to Podunkville without his violin, she got her job here and has supported him ever since."

"How come nobody ever uses his name? What is it?"

"Julian. I guess it embarrasses most folks. He's always called Polly's husband. . . ."

When I thanked her and started to leave, she stopped me.

"How come, if you're really an ex-convict, you were a cop awhile?" she asked.

"Well, convicts can get over it," I said. "You serve your time, you're supposed to be even."

"So if you were a cop why're you a sign painter now?"

"That was a temporary job—I just filled in awhile."

"From what we hear, you were awful good at it—why're you just on the road again?"

"It gives me a chance to meet new people—"

"If it was me," she said firmly, "I wouldn't think it worth the time in places like Podunkville."

"Well, I met you here."

"I doubt that's worth the trip," she said.

"How'd you get along with Ecke?" I asked.

"He didn't give me any trouble, I didn't give him any sass. Mostly I'd say he was fair and reasonable to work for. I know he rubbed lots of people the wrong way—"

"Like Alexander?"

"Alexander wouldn't admit liking anybody who's over him—but he wasn't one of the Ecke haters. And if he killed anybody, it'd be with a prescription."

"Professional pride?"

"Something like that."

"Will you have lunch with me?"

"You buying?"

"Sure."

"Come around at twelve."

7

It WAS ALREADY 11:30 A.M., so I drifted over to Leslie's Café and chinned with Jim about touching up the sign out front, which had faded with sun and tough weather. He finally agreed it could stand it and settled on five bucks for the job. Then I asked what he knew of the Ecke clan. He said far as he knew, the kids got along just fine with Evadne and never resented her replacing their mother.

"Olivia was a good woman, but none of the kids exactly worshiped her. Now I've said that bad, but I hope you get my meaning. I'm trying to say she was, well, edgy and kind of wrapped up in herself, you know?"

"And Evadne isn't?"

"Oh, no. And smart. Never tried bossing the older two when she moved in. Right off treated 'em like equals. Maude, their hired girl, says part of the reason old Ecke got so mad at his young wife was 'cause the kids took her side against him when they had fights."

I went to the drugstore at noon and walked Elaine back the half block to the café under the blazing sun. Hot wind whipped her full skirt and swirled dust along the high curb. Across the street a guy stopped and stared at us just before we went inside.

Jim's eyebrows lifted a notch as he watched us taking a booth along the east wall. The young waitress who came to our table grinned secretively at Elaine.

"You got a regular boyfriend?" I asked Elaine after we'd ordered and the waitress left.

"No. There's a fella thinks he should be but he's not."

By the time we got our sandwiches and coffee several more people had come into the place, and there was a steady murmur of talk. Most new arrivals looked our way once or twice before elaborately turning their attention to each other and the menus.

Elaine pointedly ignored the gawkers and lifted her chin a notch.

"Don't overdo it," I told her.

"What?"

"Letting folks know you don't care what they think. They might get the notion you're with me in spite of them, not because I'm such a great guy."

She lowered her chin some and frowned.

"I don't care what they think. It's none of their affair who I lunch with."

The man I'd noticed across the street came in. He was red-haired, husky, no taller than me, and some younger. After giving me the once-over he went to the counter, took a stool, and watched us in the mirror on the west wall.

I tipped my head his way.

"That the fella thinks you should be his steady?"

"No," she said after a quick glance. "That's his friend, Pinky. He keeps an eye on me."

"How come?"

"Because Bud, the would-be boyfriend, works in Aquatown and only gets back here weekends."

"He scare other fellas off?"

"Any he can scare off I wouldn't want."

"You like tough guys?"

"Not especially. But a guy who could be scared off wouldn't be interested enough to bother with."

"I guess you're a pretty demanding woman."

She gave me a grin for the first time. "Does that scare you?"

"Not much."

"I don't think much of anything scares you, does it?"

"Oh yeah. Typhoons, rattlesnakes, and managing women."

"Well, you've nothing to worry about but the last around here."

"That's usually the case."

Walking her back to the drugstore, I told her we really needed to know where Ecke had been driving to the night he got killed. She frowned in thought and said it might have been Aquatown. He went pretty regular, and while sometimes he had business there, because he owned property on the west side, he seemed to go at odd hours and even stayed overnights now and then.

"Ever give an address where you could reach him?"

"He might've told Alex. I never heard."

Alex was behind the prescription counter when I drifted back his way. He gave me his owlish look and said I was too old for Elaine. I said I didn't realize he was her father. He snorted.

"She tells me the boss hit Aquatown regular, sometimes stayed overnight. You know what hotel he used?"

"What the hell's that got to do with him getting killed in Podunkville?"

"We don't know, do we? Why're you being cute about it?"

He glowered a second, then said, "The Bingham. He was a silent partner in the place. Had problems with it because the partner, Bingham, hired a twit son-in-law as manager and the guy objected to Ecke bringing in girlfriends. Said it'd ruin their reputation."

"Thanks a million."

Officer Hurlbut wasn't in his office when I went there, and it took about ten minutes to locate him at the pool parlor. He'd been chinning with the proprietor and introduced me as the man from Corden helping out on the Ecke murder case. The proprietor's name was Durfee. He looked me over and grunted.

"I thought he'd be bigger," he said to Hurlbut.

"He's big enough," Hurlbut assured him.

"I might have something," I said.

"Hope it's nothing catching. Okay, we'll cover it."

He told his buddy good-bye, and we went out in the sun and dust.

I told him about Ecke's travel to Aquatown and where he stayed.

"Well, that's fine. I'll call them up."

"Maybe it'd be better face-to-face. If he was into hanky-panky, we might get more from the chambermaids than the desk clerk."

"You want to go talk to them?"

"You pay expenses?"

"I got nothing to pay expenses with."

"Okay—I'll call Lieutenant Baker, see if he'll help."

He had no objection to that, and a few minutes later I was talking with Baker. He gave me a hard time for not sticking with what I could handle, like a paintbrush, but agreed to send a man around to ask a few questions after he got the full story of Ecke's murder. Said to call back in the morning.

I ate supper at the Widow Bower's and afterward went around back and remounted the last two tires on my Model T. All the while I kept taking sneaky peeks at the Ecke place. Once I saw Terrell watching from an upstairs window and another time caught Jennifer staring through the kitchen window.

When the car was ready to roll, I built a cigarette and smoked it while watching the house openly. About the time I finished the cigarette Terrell came out the back door and headed for me.

"Why're you spying on our place?" he demanded.

"Just looking," I said. "It's a fine house."

"You're making Jennifer and Ev nervous."

"Ev? I didn't see her look out."

"She's got problems enough without you snooping around. So's Jennifer."

"It was you moved the car and took the tires off, wasn't it?"

His mouth sagged, then tightened. He clinched his fists.

"No, it wasn't, but what if I did?"

"All I really care about is, was it your own idea or did your pa tell you to do it?"

"Hah!"

"Does that mean you wouldn't do anything he told you, or what?"

"I didn't hop anytime he whistled."

"Even if you liked the tune?"

"Just leave us alone. Nobody ever did anything to Dad until you came to town, and if we had a cop with any brains you'd be in jail."

"Where were you Tuesday night?"

"None of your goddamn business."

He wheeled and marched back to the house.

I hitched up my pants, gathered my tools, stored them in the Ford, and rolled another cigarette.

Jennifer came out the back door and walked slowly my way. She was wearing a light-colored housedress that fit her loose and proper as a matron's uniform.

"Terry was in his room Tuesday night," she said.

"All evening?"

"Yes."

"And so were you, huh?"

She nodded. Her eyes were steady and calm.

"Did he get a telephone call around nine-thirty or ten?"

She shook her head and then said no firmly.

"His bedroom on this side of the house?"

Her answer followed an eye-blink's pause.

"Ye-e-es . . ."

"And being a warm night, the window was open, right?"

She conceded that.

"So he could've heard the little back-and-forth between his dad and me?"

"He wouldn't pay any attention to something like that. He plays his radio all the time in there and wouldn't hear talk outside."

"Where's your room?"

"Just down the hall from his."

"So you could've heard too."

"I didn't."

"Your dad ever talk with other people staying at the widow's?"

"He might have. I never sat around just waiting to hear things."

"Ever see your dad hit your ma?"

"No."

"But you saw her bruised, right?"

"That was a long time ago. Why ask about that?"

"Trying to find out why somebody killed him. Don't you want to know that?"

She only stared at me.

"You ever see him hit your stepmother?" I asked.

"Evvie wouldn't kill him. She wouldn't hurt anybody."

"What made him get mad?"

She tilted her head back, as though stretching her neck, and after a moment lifted her hands to her face, touching her cheeks.

"All kinds of things. A wrong question, speaking too low, answering too sharp, doing any job clumsily or stupidly. Dad was terribly smart and stupidity made him wild. He had no patience."

She fell silent, folded her arms under her small breasts, and hugged herself as though cold, although the air was warm and the wind still at the moment.

"I'd guess it was a tough house to grow up in," I said.

"There were bad times. But it wasn't always like that. He brought presents when we were little and took us to the lake and out fishing and for rides—"

"And you were always his favorite."

"I suppose so. Being older I seemed smarter than the others, and learned early how to appease and please him. He never hit me."

"How about Terry?"

"Terry didn't kill him. He was too afraid. It wouldn't have occurred to him."

"So when his father called and told him to move my car and take off the wheels, he did it, right?"

"Is that terribly important to you?"

"If you mean, does it make me mad, no, it's the kind of stunt I'd have pulled when I was his age. But I want to know who did it and when so I can figure out if it had anything to do with your father's murder."

"You won't do anything to Terry if I tell you?"

"You've already told me, but no, I won't even squawk."

"Okay, I'm trusting you. Terry did hear you talking with Daddy and went out and took your wheels off."

"All by himself?"

"He made Baxter help."

"Where was your stepmother?"

"Up in her room. That's on the opposite side of the house, so she didn't hear anything."

I thanked her for leveling with me and asked if she'd go a step further. She said maybe.

"Did you know about your dad messing with other women?"

"I heard stories, and like I said, he was gone lots, so I thought they could be true."

"You know about Polly Astor?"

"I didn't really know."

"How about someone else, newer?"

She seemed to wilt a little.

"I guess there had to be someone in Aquatown."

"But you don't know who?"

"No idea."

"Your dad have friends there he was close to?"

"Yes. Avery Hamel. He runs a drugstore there. They went to conventions together and shared lunches a lot, I think."

"What's he call his drugstore?"

"Hamel's."

I decided to visit Aquatown one way or another.

8

It WAS OVER a hundred miles from Podunkville to Aquatown, and I spent a while figuring a way to pay for it. The
only prospect that came to mind was the fresh widow.

Granted, it was a boneheaded notion, but hunches have
always served me better than brainpower, and I went over to
Ecke's place just as if it made sense.

Evadne was in the backyard looking at a patch of straggly
hollyhocks by the porch, and while my showing up didn't
light any flares in her eyes, she greeted me politely enough.
I called her Mrs. Ecke, and she suggested I use Evvie since
everybody else did, including the kids.

I explained my idea of talking with people in Aquatown
and the problem of finances.

She studied me for several seconds, probably trying to
decide whether I was a nut or just too eager for some of her
inherited money to resist making a wild shot at sharing it.

I told her I'd talked with the top cop in Aquatown about
getting some follow-up, but since the killing didn't happen
in his town, it wasn't likely he was going to throw the whole
force into action for my benefit.

"That's interesting," she said. "I'd been thinking of a trip
to Aquatown. Could you drive the Packard?"

"Well, uh, sure."

"We couldn't just the two of us go. There'd be talk. I'll ask
Jennifer along."

With a little effort I managed to look uneasy about the

responsibility for two women and suggested Terry should come along.

"No. He'd be bored and that makes him dreadful company. We can't go today because the funeral's this afternoon. Let's plan tomorrow."

"Whatever," I said.

"We'll go in the morning, spend the night at the Bingham Hotel, and come back Friday."

At supper that night the Widow Bower told me it seemed half the town turned out for Ecke's funeral. A good many of the folks looked solemn, but only Polly Astor really wept.

"I suspect," said Jack, her young boarder, "that people like her suffer most at a funeral because they never had a real hold on the loved one. The way family does, I mean."

The widow looked distressed by such a notion, but Billie grinned and said he hit it right on the snout.

"Women who go after other women's husbands are all alike. Born losers, weepers. Serves 'em right."

"How'd the sons and daughters act?" I asked.

"About as you'd expect," said the Widow Bower. "Jennifer was a perfect lady, composed and motherly toward the other children and even Evvie. Terry looked sullen, as usual. Pauline was sort of melancholy but awfully interested and looking around. I got the feeling she was counting the house. They stared a little when she saw me. Probably thought I'd not come since she knew her father and I had no love for each other. Baxter was thoughtful. He's a strange quiet boy, I guess I feel sorriest for him. He's overpowered by Jennifer, who's always in control, and I'm sure Terry bullies him something awful. Even little Pauline seems to intimidate him in a way—"

"She's a little minx," said Billie with satisfaction.

"I was surprised to see you at the funeral," the widow said, turning to Jack. "Had you ever met Mr. Ecke?"

"Oh yes." He nodded. "We were at planning meetings several times. He was a good politician, whatever kind of father he may have been. Talked sense and people listened.

I heard he was planning to get into state politics, run for the legislature maybe, and I think he'd have done okay."

"In spite of his womanizing?" demanded Billie.

"Well, he wouldn't have been the first or last politician with that weakness."

Jack and I went outside together after supper, and I asked how Evvie handled herself at the funeral.

"Very proper," he said. "She wore a veil that hid her face, but she kept her head down and acted the way you'd expect a fresh widow to. Why, do you think she wasn't exactly brokenhearted?"

"I didn't expect she'd throw herself on the casket."

He grinned and watched me roll a cigarette.

"I heard she's going to run the drugstore," he said.

"Yeah? Where'd you pick that up?"

"Talking with Alex after the funeral. Asked him what'd happen to his job. He said the missus had already assured him his job was secure and she was keeping Polly and Elaine on too, if they were willing."

"You think Polly'll be willing?"

"She will if she does as her husband wants."

I got my smoke going and squinted at him.

"You seem pretty in touch with the town. How long've you lived here?"

"Just over a year. I grew up in Minneapolis, and this was quite a change but I like it. In a small town you can see what's going on so clearly it's almost like watching one of those ant castles with the glass walls—you know?"

"Ever think you might go into politics?"

"Only from the back rooms." He grinned. "I'm not the kind to run up front. Public speaking scares me stiff."

"You know who Ecke's Aquatown sweetie was?"

"No. But everyone's sure he had one."

"He owned property there, I hear."

"That's the story. Couple duplexes and an apartment house. You going downtown?"

I said yes, and we began walking north toward the business district. I asked if he knew how Ecke came by the properties.

"From his father. I understand he ran a real estate business."

"You know if Jennifer Ecke's got a guy?"

He laughed easily. "Come on, I don't know everything about this place."

"Got a girl of your own?"

"I play the field."

"Tried Elaine?"

"At the drugstore? No, she's a bit prickly for me. I guess you don't mind that, eh? Hear you took her to lunch."

"You really do keep track."

He grinned and said, in this town what else did a man have to do for a hobby? He went into the soda fountain, and I traveled on to the pool hall.

Durfee wasn't friendly when I found him at the end of the bar overlooking the pool tables. It seemed possible he'd heard stories about my work with a cue. I got a beer, and after a time a paunchy half-pint with a pouty mouth and no hair to mention invited me to go a round and was good and lucky enough to win two games. I didn't notice him getting cocky, but while I was lining up my last shot, Durfee called him over and talked to him real low. My shot didn't go, and he came back, sank the two remaining balls, and gave me a kindly smile.

"Bet on the next one?" he asked.

"Why not?"

I saw Durfee scowl and guessed his boy had ignored advice offered by the proprietor.

It was a good game. We both made some unlikely shots and muffed a couple sure things. He was better than average at leaving no setups, and for a while it looked like all either of us was doing was trying to keep the other guy from dropping a ball. I got the last two in spite of him.

"Wanna up the ante?" he asked, not offering to pay off.

He won the fourth round and suggested another boost in the ante.

"You sure?" I asked.

"Why not?"

"Because Durfee told you I was hustler."

"That don't make you no magician. I can take you."

"Okay. But if I win we just call it even."

That surprised him, so he looked at Durfee. The man nodded and he said okay.

He took the break and got four balls before I got a turn. I dropped three and missed the fourth. He finished the table and was so happy he bought me a beer.

Durfee was so proud he drank one with us.

I've found all the world loves a winner except the losers and it can pay to lose in the right place at the right time.

$\triangledown$

9

We left Podunkville in the Packard at nine the next morning with Evadne and Jennifer in back and me up front like a chauffeur. They chattered away as if they were old classmates instead of stepmother and daughter while I concentrated on appreciating the car. It was the biggest, slickest I'd ever been in, let alone driven.

When we reached Redfield, Evadne suggested we stop at a restaurant for coffee, and there was no problem parking in front or getting a booth.

As we settled with our brew and fresh doughnuts, I asked Evadne where her name came from.

"It's Greek. Father taught Greek history, and Evadne means 'faithful unto death' and he liked that. The first thing that impressed me when I met Basil was he knew my name's meaning and asked if I knew the meaning of his. I said 'royal.' He was very impressed." She grinned. "I didn't tell him it'd been my father's name. I guessed his father must be a Greek teacher too, but he was only a businessman who'd been a terribly bright college boy."

"How'd you meet?"

She laughed.

"At the Nicollet Hotel in Minneapolis. There was a druggists' convention, and I was a hostess with the hotel and wore a name badge. Basil saw it, stopped me, and started talking names, and it was such a switch on approaches I agreed to have dinner with him and it just sort of went from there."

"You went home with him from Minneapolis?"

"Oh, goodness no, it wasn't that quick. But he called me every night. I was suspicious that he had a wife at first, but after a couple of weeks he came back to town for a long weekend and showed me pictures of his family and a newspaper clipping about his wife's funeral. He was very sensitive about things and guessed I didn't trust him, although I never really admitted I was suspicious because I thought it'd make him angry. I learned early he had a temper. He never lost it with me before we married, but I saw him get mad at other people. He terrified waiters and cabdrivers, people who'd always scared and managed me, so I found it exciting."

I watched Jennifer for reactions to this line. Her serene face never changed; she watched with a kindly smile, nibbled her doughnut, and sipped the bitter coffee.

"He never asked me to marry him," Evadne said. "One day he pulled a little box from his pocket, opened it to show me the ring, and asked what I thought of it."

She put her hand on the table and wiggled her ring finger, showing off the rock I'd noticed before since it seemed big enough to make lifting the hand an effort.

"I told him it was too extravagant. He grinned and said, 'Maybe even vulgar?' Then he told me to try it on. I did and he said, 'It only looks vulgar on other people.' I had to laugh, because of course that's how it seemed. I've worn it ever since."

"How long was it after your marriage when he hit you the first time?"

Her face, which had been all animation, suddenly turned wooden, and she glanced at Jennifer apologetically. Jennifer patted her forearm and moved her head in something not quite a nod.

"It must have been almost half a year," said Evadne, looking into space.

"Did it become a habit?"

Her face and voice turned bitter.

"In the last year it was more like he made a practice of it."

Jennifer's expression didn't change, but I began to wish

she'd stayed home. It was plain she knew what had gone on but wasn't used to sitting around listening to tales of her father's meanness.

When we left Redfield, both women sat in front with me. Jennifer was in the middle.

I asked if she knew Jack Springer. She glanced at me and said yes.

"Has he dated you?"

She nodded.

"Pretty often?"

"Not awfully."

"How'd your father feel about you going with him?"

"He didn't like it."

"Did he try to stop you?"

"Yes."

"How?"

"He told Jack he'd lose his job if he persisted."

"Could he manage that?"

"Probably. He had a lot of influence. Jack believed him, I think, but we still saw each other."

"On the sly?"

"Yes."

"Were you together Tuesday night?"

She said no, but I wasn't sure I believed her.

I asked what her father had against Jack, and she said it ranged from his being too old for her to having no financial resources or prospects. The words, I guessed, were quoted from her father, and she added that he had never approved of any boy or man who'd been interested in her.

We checked into the hotel a little after noon. They shared a room on the fourth floor; mine was on the sixth.

Before they took the elevator, I made an appointment to meet them in the lobby at five-thirty and then headed down to the police station and visited Lt. Baker.

He was about as cozy with me as when I'd been his favorite suspect, but after some sparring around told me Ecke had room 416 at the Bingham Hotel the weekend before he was murdered. Came in Friday night, left about Sunday noon. Had no announced visitors, and no one knew if he'd come in early or late. He was a familiar guest, not too popular even though he tipped well.

"You know who did his room?" I asked.

"No, I don't, and don't give a damn. He didn't die here or commit any crime I know of, so I didn't fingerprint the room or interview the whole goddamn hotel crew. You asked me to check was he at the Bingham. I sent a man around, he got the room number and dates. What the hell more'd you expect?"

"I'm glad you didn't waste any time or effort," I said, thanked him for his beautiful cooperation, good intentions, and sweet nature, and said good-bye. He suggested I go do the impossible and went back to work.

At the hotel I found two maids doing up rooms down the hall from room 416, wrapped a dollar around my first two fingers on the right hand, and said I'd appreciate a little information if they'd be so kind. The greenback made them kind, and I learned yes, they had done room 416 the past weekend and it seemed more than one person had used the bed and bath. One even admitted she saw a woman leaving the room Sunday morning and claimed she reported it to the management.

I went down to the desk and asked for the manager. The clerk was so reluctant I thought the man must be shy as Cinderella before she got the glass slipper, but when he finally showed he was strictly the supercilious sonofabitch type. His hair was patent leather, his cheeks chipmunk full, and his mouth prissy. His approval of my looks and garb was total.

I tilted my head toward a vacant corner of the lobby and said we should talk. He evidently thought nobody'd see us there, so he went along and sat down after carefully tugging up his pants to preserve the razor crease.

"You've got a nice place here," I said, "and I can see you're a nice guy so I'm going to do you a favor."

"Yes?" The tone was frigid.

"You had a guest last week, Mr. Ecke."

His expression became guarded.

"Of course. As I told the other officer, a tragic loss—"

"He took a room for one, right?"

"No, he was here two nights. . . ."

"I meant one person."

"Oh. Yes. Of course."

"But he shared it with a woman."

He looked quickly around the lobby and seeing no one close, returned his slightly pop eyes my way.

"Where'd you hear that?"

"We know it, so do you. Okay. Mr. Ecke was a big man, a steady guest, a free spender. So we won't worry about dirty little details, right? But the man's been murdered and we need to know some things. I want the name of the woman."

"That's all?"

"That's all."

"All I know is her first name. Lola."

"She got a husband?"

"I don't know. I doubt it."

"She young?"

He shrugged, looking superior.

"A floozy?"

"I've never seen her. I just heard from the help. . . ."

"Did the help say how she was dressed?"

"No. He recognized her. She's a woman of certain advantages."

"She wasn't a floozy?"

"She wouldn't have got in if she were. This is a highly respectable hotel."

"Okay. She dressed like she had money, that's what it takes, right?"

"Well, you don't want to offend a certain class of people in our business. You have to be very discreet."

I got up and said he was a very bright man who ought to go far. He said he hoped he could trust my discretion but couldn't make it sound convincing. I gave him another hypocritical smile and left.

10

AVERY HAMEL'S PHARMACY didn't have the six-foot-high shelves that made Ecke's Drug a mess of tunnels. Goods were lined on three- to four-foot-high shelving that let you look across the place and see customers and clerks. The overhead lighting made labels readable, so you didn't have to wait for your eyes to adjust when you came in from the sunny sidewalk.

The pharmacy counter was along the west wall, and I ambled over and greeted a tall, balding man with wire-rimmed glasses who rose from a desk and peered at me over the lens tops.

"I just came to town with Basil Ecke's wife and daughter," I said. "They say you and Mr. Ecke were close."

He blinked, tilted his head back enough to eye me through his glasses, and nodded.

"Who're you?"

I told him and said I'd been helping Officer Hurlbut check out some angles on the killing.

"You're his deputy?"

"Let's say I'm an unpaid helper."

"Working for Evvie?"

"Just helping out."

"I see. Just a Good Samaritan."

"Actually I'm more Irish, English, Scotch, and French."

"But good," he suggested. His smile only showed in his blue eyes.

"Not bad. Would you mind talking about your friend?"

He gave that a second's thought, then called to a man in a room beyond the back wall, who came out with a questioning look.

"I'm going over to Mac's place—be back in a bit."

He lifted a section of the counter, came out, and nodded me toward the front door. He walked with his bald head thrust forward and his long arms dangling.

"I've noticed," he said, "that all sorts of people want to help Evvie. You think it's her good looks or does she just bring out our parenting instincts?"

"Some of each," I said.

"Her talent in that line often offended Basil. He thought she worked too hard at it."

We entered a small café, drifted to a back booth, and he settled down with a sigh. A waitress followed us and asked what I'd like. She didn't have to ask him. I ordered coffee.

"How do you like Mrs. Ecke?" I asked as the waitress left.

"I thought you wanted to talk about Basil."

"I wanted you to."

This time the grin reached his mouth, showing small, uneven teeth.

"You don't seem all shook up about his death," I said.

His face sobered and turned thoughtful, as though I'd revealed something strange to him.

"Interesting. You're right. I enjoyed Basil. He was very intelligent, energetic, and at times stimulating—but he wasn't a man you warmed to. I can't be sentimental about him. Oh, I'll miss him at conventions and be sorry he won't drop around for a coffee now and then, but the fact is he rather exploited our relationship—pretended we were old cronies, getting together at the local bar and all that, when mostly he was out hustling high-classed hussies. I told him eventually it'd get him into serious trouble, but Basil was the last man to take well-meaning advice. His randy forties expanded into his fifties, and he wasn't a man to deprive himself of anything he wanted. And he wanted young women desperately."

"Know who he was with at the Bingham Hotel last weekend?"

"I assume it was Gloria Altman."

"What about Lola?"

"I don't know about any Lola. Where'd you hear of her?"

"Can't remember," I said, looking him straight in the eye. "What can you tell me about Gloria Altman?"

"Typical Ecke pick. Young, good-looking, married to a car dealer who makes good money but spends too much time with his poker pals to keep track of his wife."

He told me his name was Harry.

I drove the Packard over and parked on the street before Harry's lot. A young salesman strolled my way, taking in the car and me, trying to decide if I'd stolen it.

I asked for the boss, and he led me into the showroom and entered a small office. A moment later a husky, dark man with sleek hair and a chin slick as enamel came out, trailed by the salesman, and regarded me with narrowed eyes.

"He came in a new Packard," the salesman said.

Altman looked through his front window at the car.

"Where'd you get that?" he asked me.

"Mrs. Ecke."

"Ah," he said. "She want to sell it?"

"Might."

"Let's look her over."

We left the salesman and walked in silence toward the car. The sun was hot, and we both squinted against it. When we were at the curb, he stopped and folded his arms.

"So—you a cop?"

"More like a private. You know where your wife was last weekend?"

"That's my business."

"Murder makes it my business."

He stared into the car, unfolded his arms, took a cigarette

pack from his shirt pocket, shook one loose, and stuck it in his face.

"I was in Sioux Falls. My wife was home, I'd guess. You think I should ask her?"

"If you don't, I'll have to. Or maybe you'd rather Lieutenant Baker handled it."

He shrugged.

"Who saw you in Sioux Falls?" I asked.

"You want a list?"

"Just the ones you spent time with."

"I can give you that."

"Fine. Where were you Tuesday night?"

"At the legion hall."

I asked from when to when, and he got vague. I said it'd be handy if he could give me names of guys who'd seen him around from say eight-thirty to ten-thirty that night. He didn't like it, but another hint that maybe Lt. Baker would be an alternative brought him around. He went back in his office with me along and jotted down two lists of names.

"Do me a favor," I said as I left. "Don't try to call these guys and tell them what to say. You don't know who I'll see first and you probably can't reach them all on time, and in the long run it'll save both of us time if you just sit tight."

He didn't like it but only claimed he had nothing to worry about and wouldn't dream of calling any of them.

I didn't believe him, and he probably didn't expect me to.

$\triangledown$

11

I GOT ALTMAN'S home number from the directory and called. The answering voice was hardly a murmur.

"Mrs. Altman?" I asked.

"Mmn."

"I've just been talking with your husband. Checking up on the Basil Ecke murder. Will you be home for the next hour or so?"

That got me silence.

"Mrs. Altman?"

"Who are you?"

I gave her my name.

"I've already talked with the police." The voice became distinct with annoyance.

"Yeah, I know, but you never get through till the case is closed. I'm on my way over, okay?"

There was more silence, and when I said her name again, she told me she'd be home and hung up.

It took a while before she answered my knock and slowly opened the inside door. Her eyes flickered past me to the Packard out front and widened.

"Recognize the car?" I asked.

She took a deep breath, pushed the screen open, and waved me inside.

She was dark and slender in an expensive deep green dress, golden earrings, and classy high-heeled shoes. I guessed she hadn't been out of high school more than five years. She led me into a wide living room with a thick carpet in a few thousand colors that covered the floor almost to the walls. The couch and easy chair set were blue, two maroon chairs and a dinky table with a vase of flowers were in front of the couch. The flowers were something white with a single red one in the center. She took the blue easy chair and sat with her feet together and her hands dangling over the chair arm ends.

"I hear you were with Mr. Ecke last weekend," I said as I parked on the couch near her.

She stared at me with her mouth barely open. Then she recovered, closed her mouth tightly a moment, and leaned forward.

"Where was I supposed to be with Mr. Ecke?"

"At the Bingham Hotel."

She looked pained and drew back. "Really? But I wasn't, you know. Basil had a new love. You'll have to talk with her to find out what happened last weekend. I wasn't involved."

"Who is she?"

"You don't know? I thought everyone did. Her name's Lola. Lola Bishop."

"You know her?"

"Oh yes, only too well."

"Is she married?"

"Yes. Her husband's in prison. A swindler and a thief. They're a lovely couple."

The sarcasm was bitter as green beer.

"She was a friend of yours once, huh?"

"Well, I see you are a detective. Yes, we were classmates at Aqua High. Inseparable once. I introduced her to Basil at the Bingham bar, if you can imagine. I actually watched him starting to lust for her—probably the most humiliating experience of my life. She had the gall to apologize to me after she heard—"

Suddenly she brought her hands up to her face, bowed her head, and began to cry.

"Your husband know what went on?" I asked after a moment.

She shook her head.

"You're sure?"

She found a handkerchief in a pocket of the classy dress, wiped her eyes, and after a moment raised her head.

"He does and he doesn't." She dabbed at her nose, got up, and walked out, saying she'd be right back. I heard her go upstairs and guessed she made a visit to the bathroom to repair her face. I looked around some, moved into the hall, and walked to the kitchen. It was all modern with a new gas stove, Frigidaire, and built-in cabinets. The floor was covered with gleaming tiles.

She came back down the stairs, frowned as we met in the hall, and led me back into the living room.

"Was your husband home Tuesday night?" I asked.

"No. He was at the legion hall."

"Is that a regular Tuesday thing?"

"It's a regular thing any night, just about."

"So you were alone here?"

"Yes."

"When'd you hear about the murder?"

"Wednesday morning. Lola called to tell me."

"Where'd she hear?"

"I never asked."

"Did you talk long?"

"What difference does that make?"

"I'm trying to find who killed the guy, and that means I've got to find out all I can about anybody who'd want him out of the way. That includes jealous boyfriends, girlfriends, and what have you. Get the picture?"

"Yes. You want to know if Lois had any boyfriends that'd be mad at Basil."

"You got it. Or if she had any reason to be sore at the guy herself. He liked to smack women around—did he ever hit you?"

"No, of course not. I don't believe Basil'd ever strike a woman."

"He did it all right, but maybe only to ones he married. I know he hit Evadne."

"Well, she probably asked for it."

"Did he talk about her to you?"

"He talked to me about everything. That's why we got on so well—we had no secrets—"

"Until Lola."

"Yes, until her."

Just when I thought she was going to turn on the water-works again, the front door opened and Harry Altman came barging in.

"What've you told him," he yelled as his wife came to her feet in alarm. "This sonofabitch is no cop—he's a snoop—"

I've never believed in discussion when a man's coming my way with murder in his eye and both fists tight, especially when he's bigger than I am. His first haymaker sailed over my head as I went under, and his momentum carried him beautifully when I straightened up and dumped him on the couch. He rolled off, still willing, and I buried one in his belly, which folded him over to meet my rising knee. A nice rabbit punch was the final tranquilizer and dropped him peaceful as a kitten on the carpet.

I was some surprised the wife didn't scream. I turned her way to find her standing with clenched hands at her cheeks and wonder in her eyes as she stared at Harry on the carpet.

"He's okay," I assured her. "You got any whiskey?"

She crossed her fists over her breasts and stared at me.

"You want a drink?"

"I think he might when he comes around."

"Oh. Yes, of course." She unclenched her hands and walked calmly into the hall and toward the kitchen.

The battler stirred on the carpet, rolled to his side, and slowly sat up. He didn't look at me.

"You called Lieutenant Baker, huh?" I asked.

He nodded and gingerly examined his nose, then the back of his neck. He got a little blood from the nose. I went to the door, met his wife coming back with a quart bottle, took it from her, and suggested she get a wet washcloth to sponge off her hubby's nose.

She obeyed politely.

"You want a shot?" I asked Harry, who was still sitting on the floor but had straightened his legs and was leaning against the couch.

He took it and held the bottle with both hands for a moment.

"Don't try swinging it," I said. "You'd just lose a lot of good booze."

He looked at me and kept watching as he took a drink.

"You nearly broke my nose," he said.

"I wouldn't do anything to you you weren't trying to do to me."

He pulled up his feet and cradled the bottle.

"I guess you fight a lot," he said.

"Not usually for long."

He thought about that and nodded.

"You mind if I get up?" he asked.

"Give me the bottle first."

He handed it over, rose very carefully, and settled on the couch. His wife came in with a washcloth and wiped his nose. He looked sheepish and finally said thanks, and she went out.

"I didn't kill that sonofabitch Ecke," he said. "Would if I thought I could get away with it. Not only did he screw my wife, but then he dumped her for her best friend. I ask you, didn't he have it coming?"

"Seems like."

"Baker says you got no authority."

"Baker's always right." I lied.

"He said you're quite a guy with the ladies and I should keep an eye on my wife. That's when I came home. I couldn't believe she'd let you in."

"She thought I was a cop."

"God, she would. She tell you she'd been messing with Ecke?"

"I was working her toward it when you dropped in."

"She'd have told you. Can't keep a damned thing to herself. I don't know why I bother—"

"She's a damned good-looking woman."

"Yeah, she's that. Gloria!" he yelled.

She came to the door.

"Get us a couple glasses and some ice, will you?"

She gave him a hard look until he said please, then went back to the kitchen.

"How come you got Ecke's car?" he asked.

I explained about coming to town with Mrs. Ecke.

"Now there's a nice piece," he said, bobbing his head. "You'd think the old fart would've been happy with that. You sure she didn't knock him off?"

"Not certain. I suppose you know Lola pretty well?"

"Who, me? She's Gloria's pal, not mine."

"But she's been around here, right?"

"Well, sure, used to be—but mostly days, when I was at work. They got all this woman talk—"

Gloria returned with the ice in three glasses, and Harry thanked her very politely and poured us each a good shot. She took hers back to the kitchen.

"She puts Coke in it," he told me and lifted his glass. "So here's to crime."

I took a stiff belt from the glass and said, "There's another angle to Ecke's murder."

"Yeah?"

"Uh-huh. You know he was part owner of the Bingham?"

"No."

"Yeah. Silent partner. He and Bingham hadn't been getting along, I hear. Ecke thought the manager Bingham put in was a bum. The guy's Bingham's son-in-law, so there was some nasty goings-on between the partners. I heard the son-in-law had the jitters about old Ecke bringing women into the hotel, figured it was going to ruin the place's reputation."

"That's a laugh," he said. "Everybody knows that place is no convent."

We talked a little more before I decided I had to get on to meet with Evadne and Jennifer at five-thirty.

And Harry had given me another line to check.

$\triangledown$

12

Neither of the Ecke women were in the lobby when I got to the hotel, and spotting the chipmunk-cheeked manager behind the desk, I ambled over and admired him while he made busywork. Finally he looked up. The sight of me didn't please him any more than it had earlier. I asked if the boss was around, and he said with lofty satisfaction that Mr. Bingham was out.

"Of what?"

"The hotel," he said frostily. I leaned closer and gave him my melting grin.

"When'll he be in?"

"I presume this evening. I never did get your name . . . ?"

"Clark Gable," I said and turned away as Evadne came through the front door and hurried toward me.

"Sorry I'm late. Jennifer and I ran into people we knew and lost track of the time. What've you learned?"

I wished I could see the chipmunk's face as he took her in but I played it casual and asked where she'd like to eat.

"Let's go down the street to Wexler's—that's a nice restaurant—"

I asked what about Jennifer.

"Oh, she's eating with the friends I told you we ran into, the Rutledges. I'm famished, aren't you?"

I admitted I could manage a meal, and as we got out on the sidewalk, she told me she'd pay, it was the least she could do. That seemed fair to me.

While we ate and drank a lot of coffee, I covered most of

my afternoon, skipping the business about Bingham and
Basil being silent partners, and toned down the fracas with
Harry. Even without that, she decided Harry was the killer.

"I'll bet he lusted for Lola Bishop too, and when Basil
seduced both, it was too much for him."

"So he came to Podunkville, timed a meeting with Basil,
and did the job out back?"

"Why not? Maybe he came and hung around the garage
and heard what went on between you two and thought you'd
take the blame for the killing."

I suggested I'd ought to check out the guys he claimed to
have spent the evening with before we arranged a hanging.

When we got the bill, she slipped me money under the
table. Out on the sidewalk she asked, what next?

"I started checking Harry's alibi."

"Haven't you put in a full day?"

I shrugged.

"Let's go to a movie. I need something like that and it's
no fun going alone. You like Fred Astaire?"

I thought his dancing was okay but all the rest was pretty
awful. She said, "Come on, it'll be fun and you need a
change."

Like I said, his dancing was fine, but there wasn't enough
of it, and all the gags were about as funny as the clap, but I
couldn't help getting a kick out of Evadne's enjoyment
through the whole business. Afterward we stopped at a soda
foundation and had chocolate malts.

When she hit the bottom of hers and sucked air, making
a Scotch burp, she giggled.

"It's awful—Basil's hardly cold and here I am feeling like
a high school girl on a date. Do you think I'm horrible?"

"I think you're just free. How could you put up with Ecke
beating you?"

She looked at her empty malt glass, as if thinking she
needed another one.

"He didn't really beat me. He hit me when he lost his
temper. One blow. That always calmed him."

"You figure you had it coming?"

"No." She looked past me for a second, then made a face and met my eyes. "Well, not every time. The first times it was totally uncalled for. The trouble was, I got so sick of his high-and-mighty superiority I'd just reach a point where I had to stick a pin in his balloon. It was so satisfying to make him lose his temper because it made him feel like an ass and it was worth getting slapped to bring him off it now and then."

"How'd you get the job in the Minneapolis hotel?"

"Through my dad." The thought of him made her smile. "One of his students became pretty important there, and when I finished high school and said I wanted to go to Minneapolis, Dad talked with this man who'd kept in touch, and I was hired."

"What'd your dad think of your marriage?"

"He thought it was too hasty and never liked the idea of me marrying an older man, but he was too kind to say much. He and Mom came to the wedding, and Basil was very thoughtful of them and talked with Dad a lot. They talked about the Greeks and Romans so much you'd think nobody else ever counted."

"You ever think of leaving Basil?"

She looked at her glass again.

"I hate to admit it now, but no, not seriously." She looked at me. "I kept reminding myself how much older he was than me and how much longer women live and thought I could stand it. And I love the kids. Jennifer's really my friend and Pauline's adorable and Baxter's sweet and awfully thoughtful for a kid. Terry's a bit of a problem."

"He in love with you?"

"He thinks so, I guess. But he has no idea what to do about it. Mostly it makes him sulky."

"What'll you do if Jennifer goes to college?"

"I'll hope Terry goes the next year, or gets interested in girls his own age."

"Has Jennifer talked to you about Jack Springer?"

"Some. He's more interesting than the high school boys she knows, and she likes light petting and enjoys having a really grown man crazy about her. Great sense of power, you know? She likes to be in charge, and while Jack's mature and bright, he's no match for her when it comes down to strength of will."

"How'd she get along with her dad?"

"Unbelievable. She's the only person in his life, I'd bet, who never made him lose his temper. That worried me when I first met the family and later when I moved in, but you can't help accepting her. She may think she's superior as her dad thought he was, but has enough sense to hide it."

"Didn't they have any problem over Jack?"

"I don't believe Basil ever mentioned the man to her. Certainly she wouldn't have said anything."

"You know Basil threatened to get him fired?"

"No, but I certainly can believe it. That's exactly how he'd try to handle the problem. I hope you're not thinking maybe Jennifer killed her father. That'd be stupid. She loved him very much despite all his faults, and she's simply not the violent type. Jennifer wouldn't slap a mosquito. It's unthinkable."

Maybe to her.

$\triangledown$

13

B<small>ACK IN THE</small> hotel lobby Evadne thanked me for a nice evening and suggested we have breakfast in the hotel dining room at eight-thirty.

I said fine, got out my fixings, and began building a smoke. "Who'd Jennifer have dinner with?" I asked.

"The Rutledges and their son, Colin. He and Jennifer have always liked each other."

"How'd they meet?"

"At a summer picnic sponsored by Basil's bridge club here in town ten or twelve years ago.. The families used to get together quite often. Basil quit the club after his wife died, but Colin and Jennifer managed to meet pretty regularly through high school at dances and things. Well, good night. I imagine Jennifer's up in the room wondering where on earth I am."

After she left I went into the phone booth and thumbed through the directory looking for Lola Bishop's number. It was too late to call, but I thought I'd get it down for a try in the morning.

When I had it in my head, I looked up and saw Jennifer entering the lobby with a young man. She hugged his arm as if it belonged to her and met his dying-calf gaze with sweet understanding. I didn't get the feeling theirs was an old-family-friend relationship.

Suddenly she glanced around the lobby, and her bright blue eyes spotted me. If she felt caught, she covered it easily with a smile and a slight lift of her chin. Then she turned, gently pulled free, and murmured something. They shook hands, and he left without glancing my way.

Jennifer stopped in front of the elevator and waited as I approached.

"Was that Colin Rutledge?" I asked.

"Yes. Mother's been talking. Did she say I was smitten?"

"She said you were old friends."

"Since we were four. He's a nice boy."

"Didn't look bad."

"Have you learned anything today?"

"I'm not sure."

She smiled a smile that said she understood everything and glanced over toward two deserted chairs in a corner.

"Let's sit down a moment."

We sat. She crossed her ankles and leaned on her right elbow a little toward me.

"What sort of things have you been hearing about Daddy?"

"Probably nothing you don't know."

"You mean, like about his girlfriends and his bossy ways?"

"Some of that. Did you know he was part owner of this hotel?"

"Yes."

"Do you know Mr. Bingham?"

"We've met."

"What'd your dad think of him?"

"He didn't think he had very good judgment. They had differences."

"Like a disagreement about Bingham hiring his son-in-law as manager?"

She smiled. "You have been busy, haven't you? Yes, Daddy was very upset about that. He said the son-in-law, Mr. Clapper, was an ass."

"Did your dad ever get mad enough at business partners to belt them?"

"He wasn't emotional about business matters. In them he was quite objective. For example, on the personal level, he never liked Alex Solomon, but he's a very competent pharmacist, and Daddy tolerated his insubordination because he felt he was good for the store."

"If he was objective in business, how come he got involved with one of his employees?"

"That was sex. Daddy was never objective about sex. It rather derailed him, I'd say."

"Did he ever hit your brother Terry?"

She frowned thoughtfully. "That's interesting now you mention it. I'm sure he never did after he was too old for spanking. He bullied him a lot and made big threats, but never actually hit him any time I remember after Terry got into his teens."

"Maybe he was afraid of him."

"I don't think he was physically afraid of anything. But Terry got strong very young, and Daddy may have decided actually hitting him would lead to Terry hitting back, and he was too smart to risk either of them getting really hurt."

"And he never hit you?"

She looked me straight in the eye. "Never."

"How'd he like Colin Rutledge?"

"He made fun of him a lot. But when I got interested in Jack Springer, he suddenly decided Colin was very okay."

"Because he was no threat?"

"I suppose that was at least part of it."

"Does Jack Springer know about Colin?"

"We've never talked about him."

"How about Colin—does he know about Jack?"

"Do all these questions have anything to do with murder?"

"I never know what's connected till I ask. What about it?"

"It's possible he's heard something. He's not said anything to me about it."

"Your mother's probably getting worried about you. She expected to find you in the room."

"She's not my mother—I call her Evvie and she likes it."

"She thinks a lot of you."

"Yes. It goes both ways. Evvie's my best friend."

"Did it get to you when your dad hit her?"

"It made me sad. But I think she wanted it. She said things she knew would cause it, and she's not dumb so she must've felt a need."

"She ever flirt with guys?"

"No. That was never involved." She got a wise look and grinned at me. "She's more interested in you than anybody else who's been around."

"What makes you think so?"

"She told me there was something about you—you seemed very gentle, but terribly dangerous. She's positive you'll find out who killed Daddy."

"Well, I'll work at it."

"You really will, won't you? When I first saw you, I couldn't believe you were anything but sort of vaguely interested in finding out all about us. More curious than anything else. But you stay at things, don't you?"

"Some things. Maybe you ought to go up and ease your friend's worries."

"Am I getting too personal? Do you think I'm pushy?"

"I think you're very smart, and I'm not sure what you're after."

She laughed and got up, obviously pleased with herself.

"Good night, Carl. I hope you solve the case. I'm sure Evvie needs to have it all resolved, and I feel the same. We'll do anything we can to help."

"I'll check that out, believe me."

She gave me more of her great smile and stayed by my side to the elevator. I went to my room realizing that we both thought she'd handled herself very well.

$\triangledown$

14

WHEN I CAME down to the dining room in the morning, Evadne was already parked at a corner table and told me Jennifer never wanted breakfast so she wouldn't join us. As we were polishing off pancakes and bacon, a chubby character crammed into a gray double-breasted suit approached our table. He stopped beside Evadne, who lifted her head and frowned. His white shirt was so tight at the collar I couldn't believe he could speak, but he managed with a voice that had the tone of a gargle.

"Mrs. Ecke, my condolences. I'm truly sorry."

She thanked him and introduced me to Mr. Bingham. He hitched up his eyebrows a notch.

"You the one who asked Mr. Clapper about me yesterday?"

"Yeah. Pull up a chair."

He glanced around, as if checking to see who might disapprove of the company he was about to join. No one of obvious importance was in sight, so he pulled out a chair and perched on its edge.

"Have you found the accommodations satisfactory?" he asked.

"Okay. When'd you see your partner last?"

He glanced at Evadne.

"Don't be coy," she said, pushing her breakfast away, "I know he was your partner."

He shrugged. "I gather only I was expected to keep it secret."

"You going to answer my question?" I asked.

"Just what is your interest in this?"

Evadne spoke up. "He's helping Officer Hurlbut in the investigation. He's also worked with Lieutenant Baker, of the Aquatown police."

"I see." He didn't sound convinced. "Well, Mr. Ecke was here last weekend, and we discussed operations."

"Did that cover his beef about your son-in-law staying on as manager?"

"The subject was discussed."

"Was Clapper with you?"

"No."

"Did you see Ecke last Tuesday night?"

"No."

"Where were you that night?"

"Here. What're you implying?"

"Nothing. Just trying to get things straight. How late were you in the hotel?"

"Ten or so—maybe eleven. I don't punch a time clock, you know."

"You ever squawk about Ecke bringing company up to his room when he stayed here?"

Evadne pushed her chair back and started to rise. Bingham sprang up, almost knocking his chair over, and glared at me.

"I'm going to my room," she told him. "You two finish your talk. And don't imagine I hadn't heard about my husband's women friends. If you're wise, you'll be frank and open with Carl. Good morning."

Bingham spluttered some, but after she left, he sank onto the chair and clasped his hands on the tablecloth.

"Horrible," he muttered, "it's all a disgusting mess." He stared around the room again, looking worried.

"Maybe we could talk in your office," I suggested.

"Yes." He sighed, stood, and signaled for the waiter, who hurried over.

"Charge this table to me," said Bingham, heading for the door. I trailed along and a moment later followed him into a room just beyond the check-in counter. The dapper chip-munk I'd met the afternoon before rose from the chair behind the desk, looking worried.

"This is Wilcox," Bingham said, waving his son-in-law out of the way and moving in to sit down. "He's investigating Ecke's murder and has, believe it or not, Mrs. Ecke's blessings."

He couldn't believe it but kept his tight little mouth shut.

I picked up a chair by the wall, set it in front of the desk, and gave them the cold eye.

As he stood to the left of the desk, Clapper was about as comfortable as a grade-schooler in the principal's office, waiting for the paddle. Bingham folded his arms and tucked in his chins.

"I take it," I said, "that Ecke told you to dump your son-in-law."

"He couldn't tell me any such thing. We were equal part-ners. Since I'm an experienced hotel operator, it was ridicu-lous for him to presume he could tell me how to run this business."

"He threaten to pull out?"

"He wanted to buy me out. I wouldn't sell. This is my life. Besides, he was hurting the hotel's reputation by bringing in his harlots, it was disgraceful—"

"How many'd he bring in?"

"Two I know of. Maybe another."

"They weren't just regular whores, were they?"

"I'm not an expert in that field."

"You run hotels and you don't know about whores?"

"I've not run that kind of hotel."

I scowled at Clapper. His mouth was tighter than a snapped rattrap, and his beady eyes watched me as if he expected hell.

"Where were you last Tuesday night?"

"Here," he squeaked, and then, after clearing his throat, repeated it. "Right here. All evening. Until midnight."

"Ecke come around?"

He shook his head.

"When'd you see him last?"

"Sunday night, when he checked out."

"He owned half interest and he checked in and out?"

"No one was supposed to know he had an interest. He pretended to be a paying guest. Of course, we never billed him."

"How about his girlfriends, they check in and out?"

"We weren't supposed to acknowledge their existence."

"So there'd been an agreement, right? You'd stay on and everybody'd pretend there were no women."

Clapper looked at Bingham. So did I.

Bingham sighed. "All right. We had what they call a Mexican standoff. It was a reasonable compromise by reasonable men. We weren't satisfied, neither was he, but none of it was anything to make one of us murder the man. I admit I despised his superior attitudes and whorish ways, but I couldn't buy him out and wouldn't sell. His persecution of Dale was insufferable and only began when Dale objected to him bringing sluts to his room here. There were no complaints about his performance until that fuss. And for God's sake, look at me. Can you imagine I'd attack a man like Mr. Ecke and kill him?"

"When a man's scared or mad enough, he can do damned surprising things. And I don't think you're anybody's doormat."

He liked that. His head came up, and he lost one of his chins as he looked me in the eye.

"I was certainly mad, but not insane. Basil was a big and forceful man, and I had no weapon even if I'd thought of using one. All I could hit him with was the truth, and that hardly felled him—certainly it wasn't fatal. When he walked out of here Sunday night, we had an understanding, and I never saw him again."

I looked at Clapper.

"I never saw him after he checked out Sunday night."

I thanked him and left.

∇

15

WHEN I WENT out Evadne was in the lobby and waved me over. I told her what I'd learned. She scowled.

"Why does Bingham gripe you?" I asked.

"He's a self-important little creep who treated me as if I were feebleminded. And I'm sure he was tickled to death that Basil had a weakness for bimbos—it was the only chance Bingham had to feel superior because Basil was handsome, smart, and successful in everything he tried."

She was silent for a moment before shedding her anger and asking what I planned to do next.

"Talk with Lola Bishop."

That brought back her scowl.

"I suppose you're anxious to see what she's like."

"Yeah," I admitted. "It's hard to figure Basil looking for something else with you at home."

"Let me know if it's easier to understand when you've met her."

"That's a kind of thing I don't think anybody can understand, I mean, what makes a guy choose his women, or the other way around."

"Well," she said, "go do it. I'm going shopping."

There was no answer when I called Lola's place, so I sat in the lobby a few minutes, flipping through the newspaper, which is no way to become an optimist. About when I'd given up, Jennifer came out of the elevator, looking fresh as springwater. She spotted me at once, walked over, and smiled as I stood up.

"You seem to spend your days waiting in the lobby for me," she said.

"Only at likely times. You really skip breakfast?"

"I'm ready for coffee and maybe a doughnut."

So we went into the restaurant where I swilled more coffee, rolled and smoked a weed, and admired the way she creamed and sugared her coffee and charmed the waitress almost numb.

I asked if she knew Bingham. She said only by sight. He'd never been to their house or gone to parties they were invited to, as far as Jenny knew.

"Your dad ever talk about him?"

"No."

"So when did Evvie see him?"

"Here, I suppose. She and Daddy came to Aquatown a lot and once in a while stayed overnight."

When she'd finished the doughnut, I paid and we went back in the lobby. She asked when we'd be going back to Podunkville.

"I've still got to see someone. Your mother's shopping but I suppose'll come back around noon. How about we meet here at twelve and decide when to take off?"

With that settled I tried Lola's number again and connected. Her voice was hard-edged with a vaguely eastern accent. Yes, she was willing to see me. She gave the address of her apartment on the south side, and I wheeled over in the Packard.

She opened the door as soon as I knocked and gave me a critical once-over before letting me in.

A pink robe wrapped a frame that tapered in the middle and flared at the hips. Her eyelashes were mascaraed so thick it made her lids sag, and her lipstick was shiny on a mouth too wide and lush to seem legal.

"Did you call earlier?" she asked as she led me into a broad living room jammed with overstuffed furniture and loaded with antimacassars, fancy lamps, side tables with tasseled covers, and other junk Ma would have had if she'd married a successful thief.

I said yes.

"I was in the bathtub, and I don't hop out of that for anything but a fire alarm. So you want to know about Basil and me?"

"I want to know all I can about him."

"He was all man. I wish I'd met him before he got Evvie. Of course, I'd had a hell of a time getting rid of my husband. You know about him?"

"I hear he's in the stir."

"Well, he didn't do anything others haven't done and got away with, I can tell you that. Just had a stupid lawyer."

"He know about you and Ecke?"

"I don't know how."

"You'd be surprised what guys in stir learn about the outside."

"Well, if he did, I doubt they gave him a pass to come out and knock off Basil."

"You don't seem all broken up about the murder."

She batted her heavy eyelids to let me know I'd misjudged her. "You couldn't be more wrong. It about killed me, for God's sake—but I learned long ago a girl can't let anything that happens with men get her down for long. You can never depend on 'em in the long run. They're always running off, dying, or getting murdered. You married?"

"No."

"You got the lone-wolf look."

"How'd you know Gloria?"

"We were in school together."

"You've got an accent, sounds east."

"Lived there my last two years in high school and a little after."

"Were you with Ecke last weekend?"

"Call him Basil—Ecke sounds icky."

"Okay. Were you with him?"

"Uh-huh. I suppose one of the maids told, I know one saw me leave. They don't miss a thing."

"How'd she know your name?"

She gave me an arch look. "Well, not because I'm a regular at the hotel. This isn't that big a town, you know, lots of people know me."

"You're a woman people'd remember," I said.

"Yeah." She tried to sound sad, but her pride was plain. "So what's the diff if we played that weekend? He got killed Tuesday, wasn't it?"

"Uh-huh. Everything go fine during the weekend?"

"Right as rain. Basil was in rare form—I like to think it was a weekend to go out on and I gave it to him."

"No tiffs or spats?"

"Nary. Why would we fight?"

"Between men and women, there's always something. You ever try to talk him into getting divorced and marrying you?"

"Dearie, I may not look awfully bright to you, but I'm a long ways from dumb. He'd been tupping his woman at the store, he'd had my best friend, Gloria, and I knew he'd be after somebody new within a couple months. I wasn't about to start happily-ever-after baloney with a man like that. He gave me presents, a good time, and a little boost—I don't kid myself and reach for more than I can get. And my husband isn't in the pokey for life."

"Gloria says you called her when you heard Basil was murdered. How'd you happen to do that?"

She looked away from me and batted her eyes a couple times. With those lashes it was enough to give her a hernia. She smiled at me wearily.

"I didn't even think. The minute I heard I just picked up the telephone and called her. I knew she'd understand—"

Her voice got thick, and she became silent.

I looked around the room and realized the floor covering was almost the same as the one I'd seen in Ecke's home.

"This is quite a carpet," I said.

She sat up a little straighter and examined it.

"Yes. Basil gave it to me. The first time we were together we came here, and a week later the carpet was delivered. He didn't say a word about it until I asked if it came from him.

He was full of surprises like that. Most people think he was stuck on himself, always snotty and with his nose in the air. Well, he was smarter than anybody around—why should he pretend he didn't know it? I asked how come he decided to give me a rug, and he said because a woman like me shouldn't have a rag on her floor in case somebody wanted to make love to her there."

"Did he make use of it?"

"No. He got nervous about coming here because somebody might notice. He'd stayed at the hotel lots of times over the years so it wouldn't draw attention, and him being part owner he figured the help'd be easy to shut up. God, when that stupid Clapper made a big thing of him having me there, he turned absolutely livid. I really thought he'd kill the poor simp."

"This happen last weekend?"

"Uh-huh."

"I thought you said it was all right as rain."

"Well, between Basil and me it was. I mean, he got mad at that fool, but he didn't take it out on me. He wasn't that kind of a man."

"Who do you think killed Basil?"

She pursed her lips and made wrinkles in her forehead.

"I'd guess old Bingham or his rodent son-in-law."

"How about Harry Altman, your friend Gloria's husband?"

"Harry? Well now, he might. God knows he's got the temper, and he thinks he's a tough guy."

"You and he ever mess around?"

"Of course not! For heaven's sake, he's my best friend's husband. What kind of a girl you think I am?"

"You took her boyfriend."

"Well, that was different, he wasn't married to her, and he wasn't really good for her. The trouble with Gloria is, she takes men too seriously."

"So you were doing her a favor."

"Don't make fun—I won't pretend I went to bed with him

to save my friend, but that could've been what it came down to. I mean that I saved her."

"Could your husband have hired somebody?"

"How the hell do I know?"

"You know what kinds of friends he's got."

"No, I don't. I didn't know anything about what he was doing to get stuck in prison—he didn't tell me anything, and I didn't ask and don't want to know yet."

"A bit ago you said he didn't do anything others hadn't and got away with."

"Well, that's just what I figure and what he claimed."

"So you don't know what kind of pals he had that might have been happy to do him a favor?"

"I don't believe he knows a damned thing about Basil, and for God's sake, I hope you're not going to blab it."

"That's the least of your worries."

"It was till you showed up. I'd appreciate it if you'd go now, okay?"

I went.

$\bigtriangledown$

16

THE DESK SERGEANT sent me straight back to Lt. Baker's when I came around.

"Some folks think you're working for me," said Baker when I was seated. "Where you suppose they get that wild-assed notion?"

"No idea. I never said I was. You know Harry Altman?"

"Yeah. Why?"

"Know his wife was sleeping with Ecke?"

"No. But you do, right?"

"How about Lola Bishop? Know he was ringing her bell too?"

"No wonder he died."

"What'd her hubby get nailed on?"

"Fraud."

"He got any rough friends?"

"There were a couple. But they disappeared during his trial. Shy about subpoenas, you know?"

I dug up the list of names Altman had given me, put it on Baker's desk, and explained who the guys were.

"This is damn nice of you," he said. "You're actually going to let me in on your little job, right?"

"Unless you want everybody thinking this is my affair."

"Wilcox, your gall's an inspiration to me. You want your report in writing with maybe duplicates?"

"That'd impress Mrs. Ecke."

"No doubt. Okay, I'll check this alibi out. What the hell, I got nothing but guys sitting around waiting for assign-

·ments from an old con. What happened to the sign-painting business?"

"I got sidetracked."

"Well, go back to it. I don't want you stumbling around my territory. Who told you Altman's wife was messing with Ecke?"

"She did."

He stared at me for a moment through his thick lenses.

"You didn't come up with this while you were slipping it to her yourself, I don't suppose?"

"We were sitting in her parlor proper as an old maid and her parson. What'd you tell Harry Altman when he called about me?"

"Told him to keep an eye on his wife. He catch you at it?"

"Like I said, perfectly proper."

"So he sat down and you all had a cozy chat?"

"It wasn't quite like that."

"If you hit him, he could get you for assault."

"You had a complaint?"

He grinned, put his feet on the corner of his desk, and folded his hands behind his head.

"I'd like to've been a fly on the wall when he charged in. You handled him, didn't you?"

"He was real reasonable."

"Uh-huh. I got a tintype of that. His wife scream?"

"She was okay."

"Sure, they're all okay with Wilcox. I suppose that's how you make out so good. They know you love 'em all."

I asked if he knew the Rutledge family. His eyebrows went high enough for me to see them arch above his thick glasses.

"Why do you ask?"

"Ecke's daughter, Jennifer, had been cozy with them. Especially the son, Colin. I'd like to talk with him."

He stared at me for a moment. "What the hell you want to talk with him for? Figure he's a suspect—or that Jennifer is? What kind of dopey notion you got?"

"Just want to cover the angles. The Rutledges are money, right?"

"The old man's just the biggest lawyer in this town, that's all. Colin's gonna be another. Why'd Jennifer want to do her old man?"

"One old party claims there was incest, Jennifer admits her dad never liked her boyfriends. These things make a man think."

"That kind of talk could get a man in deep shit, Wilcox. I mean really deep."

"I haven't said anything to anybody else and won't. Just want to talk with the boyfriend a little."

"You aren't going to find him talking his head off to you like all the women seem to."

"You want to find out what Colin was doing Tuesday night?"

"No."

"So it's up to me."

"What you'll do is get your ass back to Podunkville. The sooner the better."

His telephone rang, and he picked it up with one hand while waving me out with the other. Before I closed his door, he called. I looked back, and he had his hand over the mouthpiece.

"I don't want to hear any more about you working for this office, you got that?"

I gave him a one-finger salute and left.

17

"W ILCOX?" HE SAID as I approached the hotel door.

I'd seen him slip out of an old green Chevy parked at the curb nearby. He was young, tall, wide at the shoulders, and solid through the center.

"You got me," I admitted.

"I'm Bud Elliot."

I guessed this was Elaine's jealous boyfriend but gave him a blank look and said, "So?"

"I heard you been trying to move in on Elaine. Lay off."

"Why?"

" 'Cause I told you, that's why."

I grinned at him. "You think it's that easy?"

He flushed and took a deep breath to show what a big chest he had.

"You want a cup of coffee?" I asked.

He let his air out, looked thoughtful, and finally said okay.

"Where you work?" I asked as we parked at a corner table in a small café across from the hotel.

"Parker's Bakery, in the next block."

"No kidding. My best friend's son works in a bakery in Corden. Gets you up with the chickens, right?"

"Before," he said. The waitress came, and I ordered for both of us. She was young and well shaped. We watched her walk away.

"How long you been after Elaine?" I asked.

"Since high school."

"You ask her to marry you?"

"She don't want to get married."

"And you do?"

"I wouldn't mind. You're too old for her."

"You're probably right. But you know, you can't get a girl just by clubbing the competition, even when it's old and smaller than you."

"I can't stand other guys trying to mess with her."

"She's got a mind of her own, though, doesn't she?"

The waitress returned with our coffee. He loaded his with sugar and cream while I rolled and lit a cigarette.

"It makes her real mad when I scare guys off," he confessed.

"She's not too nuts about your pal spying either."

"Yeah. That really makes her sore. I didn't tell him to do it, he just does because he's my pal."

"I'm going to tell you something you probably won't believe," I said, not sure I was going to believe it myself.

"What?"

"She had lunch with me in that café because she wanted to show you she'd go out with any-damn-body she pleased. She'd have gone with me if I was thirty years older and half her size, just to let you know she could and will. Has she dated any guys from Podunkville?"

"Not since I punched out a couple."

"Probably because she doesn't want you punching any more guys she knows well. But she wasn't worried about me because I'm a stranger. You think of that?"

"No." He scowled at his coffee and then at me. "I think maybe you're being cute."

"Why not? What's the percentage in me waltzing with you? You're younger, bigger, and more eager. It'd take a lot of work to cut you down, and I'm getting tender in my old age. Win or lose, neither of us'd gain a damned thing. You think Elaine's going to fall all over you for punching me out? You'd probably come out better if I knocked you cold and she could feel sorry for you. You got to decide whether it's worth it."

He stared at me, looked around the quite café, and sighed.

"Well, shit," he said. Then he got up and walked out. Didn't even thank me for the coffee he hadn't finished.

As I headed back to the hotel, I almost worried about getting so old I ducked a fight but instead felt a little proud of myself.

Jennifer came off the elevator as I entered the hotel lobby, and since it was only eleven-thirty, I asked how about we go visit her boyfriend, Colin.

"What for?" she asked.

"You said you wanted to cooperate. I like to check all the angles and want a look at this guy."

"We'd have to go around to the law office," she said, looking at my clothes doubtfully.

"I thought he was your age—isn't that young for a lawyer?"

"Of course. But he does some work for his father, who wants him around to see what it's all about. He even has a little office of his own."

She got up with sudden decision, and we set off. It was only a block away, one floor up. We got past a motherly receptionist who beamed at Jennifer and passed me over with only a polite, uncritical glance.

Colin scrambled to his feet as we sashayed into his cubby-hole office, got Jennifer seated, and let me find my own comfort in a straight-backed chair beside her.

Jennifer made the proper introductions and then blew my scene by explaining I was here to find out whether or not he might be a suspect in her father's murder. An ordinary guy would have been shocked numb at the suggestion, but being made of lawyer stock, he treated it as if it deserved consideration.

"I don't have a motive," he told me.

"You two got along okay, huh?"

"He wasn't crazy about me," he admitted, "but he never objected to our relationship."

"You ever hear of a rumor about Jennifer and her dad?"

He blinked and lifted his sharp chin a fraction. "What kind of rumor?"

"Incest."

Jennifer started. It was the first time I'd seen her rattled.

"What's that? Where'd you hear that?"

"In your hometown."

"It was that old witch Billie, wasn't it? The one who boards where you're staying?"

"Did you ever hear the rumor?" I asked Colin.

"No. Absolutely not. It's ridiculous. If you repeat that in public you'll regret it—"

"Sure. But keep in mind, we're messing with murder. That pretty much dumps sweetness in the sewer until the killer's caught. You ever hear of Basil Ecke beating his wives?"

"No, of course not—"

I looked at Jennifer, who was seething. "You never told him family secrets, huh?"

"Those aren't family secrets—they're malicious gossip. I brought you here because I trusted you—I never dreamed you'd start spouting every bit of filth you've heard or dreamed up—"

"I guess you two aren't as close as I thought," I said.

He looked at her; she kept glaring at me. I met her eyes, and we both knew I'd be talking to Jack Springer as soon as we got back to Podunkville.

Colin had more to say but didn't add anything useful. I said we'd best get back to the hotel, where Evadne would be wondering why we were late.

On the trip home Jennifer sat in back and pretended to sleep. Evvie sensed something was wrong, and I found it interesting that she didn't try to find out what.

$\triangledown$

18

I LET THE women out in front and drove around in back to park the Packard in the garage. As I started across the yard, Jennifer intercepted me.

"Are you going to ask Jack the same thing you asked Colin?" she demanded.

"No. He heard it the same time I did. But I'll ask if he'd heard it before and if you ever told him."

"So he got it from Billie Fielding—that witch! What'd he say when she told you that?"

"I don't remember he said anything—I wasn't paying much attention to him right then, and he left real soon."

From her expression I guessed Jack was in trouble.

"At the time he wasn't letting on to me he even knew you," I said. "There wasn't much he could say as an outsider."

Her eyes were unforgiving.

"Why can't you just drop the subject? All you're doing is spreading ugly about Daddy and me."

"I'm trying to find out who killed him."

"I don't believe it. You enjoy smearing him. You hated Daddy on sight because he was a big man with a big house and fine car and a good family—all things you've never had and never will. You're jealous!"

"That's a dandy attack, but I know better. Your old man and I aren't the same breed. The only thing I'm after is who killed him and why. Somebody tried to stick that rap on me, and I'm going to stick it back where it belongs. You ought to want whoever did it caught—instead you're worrying about me breaking eggs."

"Oh!" she cried. "You're a little monster—I hate you!"

And she ran for the house.

I thought some of going in to try to make my case, but it didn't seem likely that anything I'd dream up would make me any taller, so I gave it up and went to the Widow Bower's.

She asked me about my trip, and it was plain my stock had risen since I'd driven the Packard for the Eckes and been hobnobbing with folks in Aquatown.

I asked if anybody but Billie had ever gone for the incest story. She said there were people in town that'd go for any story and more who wouldn't speak ill of the devil. She didn't believe many took stock in poor old Billie's claims, because they knew why she was so spiteful.

Jack didn't show for supper, and I spent the meal pumping Billie for dope on her incest story. She mostly looked wise, but when I pressed hard, she got feisty and said anybody with half an eye and an ounce of sense could see it plain enough when the man doted on the daughter and she was the only one in the family he never beat up. When I pushed her on that, she admitted no, she'd never heard Pauline was bruised, but that probably meant he had long-range plans for her too.

I told her she was a dirty old woman, and she told me not a bit, she saw the world as it is.

After eating I drifted downtown and stopped by the pool hall but didn't play. At the first sight of me Durfee got a worried look, and I guessed he figured I was back to cash in on all the suckers who thought I could be taken. He asked how I liked driving a Packard, and I said it would never take the place of sex but it beat riding a mule. He laughed, and I suspected he'd heard the story about me riding a jackass backwards to a funeral back in my drinking days.

When I asked if he'd heard any bad-mouthing of Basil Ecke, he got a guarded look and admitted there'd been some.

"Like him beating his wives?"

He nodded.

"How'd he handle the kids?"

He shrugged.

"I hear Jennifer was his favorite."

"Seems like."

"Never beat her, huh?"

"Never saw any bruises."

"You know anybody had a special hard-on for Ecke?"

"Special? I don't know, outside of old lady Fielding."

"Billie?"

"Yah. She's one of the few with guts enough to bad-mouth him right out. There were plenty not too crazy about him, but he wasn't a man you wanted mad at you."

"Was there anything to Billie's claims?"

"She thought so."

"What's that worth?"

He leaned back against the bar but didn't look too comfortable.

"Well, I never heard anybody say she was an idiot or even a liar. But she does get kinda wild ideas."

"Like saying there was something unnatural between Ecke and Jennifer?"

"I never believed that."

"But you did hear it?"

"Oh yah."

"Who from?"

"It was just around."

"Like maybe from Mae Ecke?"

"Her story was old Ecke killed his first wife."

"Anybody believe that?"

"I don't think many thought he done it on purpose. More like an accident."

After that remark he said he had things to do, so I thanked him and drifted over to the drugstore, where Elaine was alone behind the counter in back.

She raised her eyebrows at sight of me.

"I was beginning to think you'd been scared off. Did you see Bud in Aquatown?"

"Yup."

She examined my face. "I guess he didn't hit you anywhere it shows."

"Never laid a knuckle on me."

"Get anywhere on your murder?"

"Probably not. How late you work?"

"Half an hour more. You going to walk me home?"

"If we take the long way."

"It won't be all the way."

"I didn't figure it would be."

She wasn't a girl who smiled a lot, but when she did it was worth waiting for. She gave me a good warmer.

"I'm glad you came."

"So am I."

The half hour passed, and we went out on Main Street, which was beginning to fill with farm families and townsfolk gathering for Saturday night revels. A few greeted Elaine and examined me with open curiosity.

"I don't guess you've painted a lot of signs since coming to town," she said.

"It's been slow."

"You make so much money when you do work that you can do as you please between?"

"No."

"But you can't let murder lay, huh?"

I shrugged and asked if she lived with her folks.

"My grandma."

"How come?"

"Ma never had a husband, couldn't handle me. Went to the Cities. Why'd you get sent to prison?"

"Because I was too drunk not to get caught."

She wouldn't settle for that, and I wound up telling her about the botched rustling and jewelry store jobs I'd tried. She got laughing about my trouble in getting the lady to lay down in the jewelry store.

"I bet she thought you had other ideas than robbery," she said.

"No. All she could think about was keeping her white dress clean."

"Why wasn't your gun loaded?"

"Bullets cost money, and I didn't plan to shoot it."

By this time we were on toward the edge of town, away from the crowds. She turned me around and started back.

"Was it awful in prison?"

"No worse than the army. Maybe better."

I tried to make her talk about herself, but she just kept steering things back to me and finally I gave up. Then we were walking up to the steps of a big house on a corner, and as she sat down on the top one of three I realized the place was deserted.

She tucked her skirt under her thighs, folded her arms, and leaned on her knees.

"You been to Minneapolis?" she asked.

"Yeah."

"Is it nice?"

"Well, sure. It's pretty big and busy but there're lakes and lots of trees and snazzy houses."

"Why didn't you stay?"

"Never thought about it. Never really thought about staying anywhere. I'm more a visitor."

"I'd like that. But it'd be hard for a woman."

I pulled out my fixings and started building a cigarette.

"Don't smoke," she said, leaning against my shoulder.

"It bother you?" I asked, tucking the tobacco sack in my shirt pocket.

"You can't smoke and kiss me."

That made sense. I put my arm around her, and she leaned into me while keeping her head down.

"That's all it's going to be," she said, "just kissing. Okay?"

"Fine."

Then she offered me her face.

She was deliberate and careful, more like she was testing a theory than getting involved. I didn't mind. Her mouth was soft and warm, her breath sweet, and after a couple kisses she put her hand on the back of my head and added a little pressure.

In a while she pulled away, turned, and lay back across my knees so she was looking up at me.

"Tell me where you've been and what you've seen."

I told her about Colorado mountains and California fruit trees, giant swells on the Pacific, beaches in the Philippine Islands, and traveling across Nebraska on a summer night in a boxcar.

"What's the most beautiful place you've ever seen?"

"You won't believe me."

"Tell me."

"You know where Summit is?"

"No."

"A little east of Webster."

"South Dakota?" She was incredulous.

"That's right. You go just beyond the town on twelve heading for Minnesota and you can see east and north just about to forever. The edge of the earth's out there, blue like the sky, all soft and beyond reach. And around you there's rolling hills covered with tall green grass the wind blows over, making it ripple like long waves and it's all alive and lovely."

"You're dreaming. The prairie's burned and dead."

"It wasn't when I saw it. Then it was green and ripe and I've never seen anything to beat it in the world."

"Have you gone back?"

"No."

She reached up and pulled me down to kiss her.

"You're afraid to go back," she said when the kiss ended. "You couldn't stand seeing it spoiled. What a sad old cowboy you are, Carl."

It was better kissing her than making an argument.

$\triangledown$

19

ELAINE'S HOME WAS a block from the deserted house where we talked and kissed. About the only places smaller than her grandma's house were ones I'd seen with a half-moon cut over the door. I kissed her again before the last good night and got a little body contact that worked me up but didn't change her mind any.

I was still thinking about her when I got back to the Widow Bower's and spotted Jack Springer sitting on the porch swing.

"You waiting for me?" I asked.

"Thought you'd be along eventually."

"Been talking with Jennifer?"

His teeth showed in the dim light as he grinned.

"I suppose you're a little sore I was cagey about her," he said.

"It made me wonder."

"Yeah. Well, I thought it'd be interesting to see how long it took you to find out."

"I disappoint you?"

"No, you did fine."

He got off the swing and suggested we take a walk. When we were far enough from the house, he said he couldn't be sure where Billie might be and he'd rather not add anything to the old lady's supply of gossip.

"You got serious plans for Jennifer?" I asked.

"Come on, Carl, you sound like her old man."

"He said that to you?"

"Pretty close. Wanted to know my prospects and intentions. I got a feeling my prospects were the most important part of the case."

"Money men put first things first."

"Jennifer's first with me."

"Where'd you meet?"

"The dance hall at Lake Kampie. She was standing with a bunch of young people and all I saw was her. Our eyes met and it was like I could hear the click. Most of the time women won't look you in the eye—you notice that? But she did. I smiled and she smiled back and I worked close and asked for a dance and she said the one after next and that was it. She floats on a dance floor. Finding out she was smart and good was all bonus—I fell for the smile and grace—do I sound sappy?"

"Some. But I can see why. So her pappy told you to lay off?"

"He did."

"Make you mad?"

"Not really. I could understand his feelings, in fact. But I was upset and scared he'd convince her to give me the gate. The way she reacted, turns out he probably did me a favor. She's not a girl you tell what to do. She'd been lots less interested if he'd approved."

"Besides not wanting him to pick her boyfriends, how'd you think she liked him?"

"Oh, till he tried to ax me he was God. All wise, good, and holy. That was clear the first night we talked. And that's why I was so surprised she defied him with me. The minute I told her he'd threatened me, she said don't give it a thought. I can handle him, that's what she said."

"You didn't worry about your job?"

"No. Ecke was big stuff in town and probably the county, but he wasn't anybody on the federal level, and that's where he had to deal if he was going to give me real trouble."

"You don't think local power's got leverage, huh?"

"Well, sometimes, sure, but even if he could get me fired

it wouldn't exactly ruin my life. I didn't want to leave here while I was still after Jennifer, but I could've worked out something. I know a few people myself."

"How'd she handle her old man?"

"They talked and he tried to convince her all he wanted was the best for her and she wasn't old enough to know what that was yet. I guess most girls'd get mad at that line, but Jen's too smart. She knew she couldn't win an open fight with him, so she pretended there was nothing serious between us and he needn't worry about her doing anything foolish and agreed she'd keep seeing that Aquatown shyster. She didn't promise to stop seeing me."

"So he left you alone?"

"Not a bit of it. I heard quick he was out to get me."

"You tell Jennifer?"

"No. It'd just upset her, and I didn't see any percentage in egging her into an open scrap with him. It'd just made him more stubborn."

We reached the edge of town, walked a block north, and started back east. Houses were mostly dark. At each corner we'd enter the glow of streetlights and soon go beyond under the overhanging limbs. We kept skirting the commercial part of town, although it being after midnight it'd certainly have quieted down with the closing of the dance hall and beer parlors.

"Why're you asking questions about Jennifer and her father?" he asked.

"You're smart enough to figure that out."

"I'm not sure."

He made that sound genuine, but we were too far from the corner light for me to catch his expression.

"How's she taken the death?" I asked.

"Better than I'd have expected in some ways. What I don't understand is, it seems like his dying's made me less important. As if it took his opposition to make her need me. I thought she'd, you know, melt in my arms, turn to me for comfort—all that. Instead she seems distant. You think she subconsciously resents the idea that I might be glad he's dead?"

"Could be."

He halted and faced me. We were in the middle of the block.

"There's something I've got to talk about. You're asking about incest. Jennifer's obsessed with that—she says it's got to stop. That's all she could talk about tonight. I think you could drive her frantic if you keep it up. Don't you like her?"

"Sure, who wouldn't?"

"Lots of people. There's envy all over town. She's too pretty, too well off, too—comfortable. People in a place like this love to think the worst of people they envy."

"I'm not spreading the story. It was here before me."

"But the death, a murder, makes people feel guilty and ashamed to bring up something like that until somebody like you—an outsider—comes around, raking it all up. Then it becomes a fact."

"I'm not blabbing it around. I asked her two boyfriends because it figured she might've said something to one of them. Most girls unload to guys they're serious about."

"Promise you won't ask anyone else."

"Well, I don't know any other guys she dated."

He wasn't satisfied with that, but after a moment he started walking again, and we went back to the widow's and our own rooms.

It bothered me some I'd been talking with Durfee about the incest question, but it didn't keep me awake.

$\triangledown$

20

NOTHING HAPPENED SUNDAY. Monday morning the Widow Bower served pancakes for breakfast, and I ate more than I needed while pumping the widow and Billie after Jack Springer left for work.

Neither knew who Ecke's money would go to. The widow assumed it'd be Evvie, but Billie said it'd go to Jennifer. I asked who was the man's lawyer. Billie said Colin Rutledge's pa in Aquatown, while the widow was sure it was a local man named Zimmerman.

I'd about finished my third cup when Hurlbut hauled his overweight carcass in and let me know he was feeling hurt I hadn't been in touch.

"You were first on my list today," I told him, and his bushy eyebrows lifted as he started stuffing his pipe. When I asked if he knew who was getting Ecke's money, he grinned so wide his big ears moved.

"You bet I do. Jennifer gets the whole caboodle. Ecke made his will right after Olivia's accident. Never changed it when he got married again."

"Where'd you get that?"

"Floyd Zimmerman, his lawyer."

As he lit up his pipe, he said he'd talked with Zimmerman two days ago. The lawyer had even suggested a few years back that Ecke ought to update his will to include Evvie, but Ecke hadn't been interested, saying whatever happened, Jennifer was fair enough to see Evvie got her share even if they weren't great pals—which they were.

I was some surprised a lawyer'd be so free with his client's business but didn't worry it any and asked if Hurlbut had any more luck than I did trying to find where Ecke'd been heading the last time I saw him. He looked sour and said no.

We left the widow's after Hurlbut had his fill of her coffee and smoked up half a book of matches trying to keep his pipe lit. The sun was already fierce by ten o'clock as we walked toward the business district, and the wind whipped dust off the graveled street, making us squint and turn our heads.

His stingy office in City Hall was hot too, but at least there was no sun or flying dust, and we sat talking over the murder. He had made up his mind some hooligan hired by Lola's convict husband had done it. That solution was handy because it eliminated all the Podunkvillites and nobody could blame Hurlbut for not being able to run down a professional killer, since it would likely be an outsider who didn't even know Ecke.

When I didn't buy that, he got huffy and claimed Lt. Baker hadn't argued when he suggested the notion during their talk on the phone. That didn't impress me, since Baker preferred simple solutions like anybody else and he'd sure never discourage a small-town cop from taking the easy out, especially if it saved him from messing around with a case that wouldn't get him any credit where he needed it.

A little before noon I left City Hall and went down to Leslie's Café. He was in the kitchen but came out when I asked for him and sat beside me while I lunched at his counter. I told him I was looking for another sign-painting job and asked if he had any suggestions who I should call on.

"Oh," he said, "the murder been solved?"

I told him about my talk with Hurlbut, and he looked skeptical but didn't argue. Finally he said I seemed to have made an impression on Durfee; maybe he'd be interested in a sign on his pool hall.

That led to a conference with Durfee, a lot of palaver over price and where I should do it. He finally went for two signs, one on each window in front, identifying it as Durfee's.

Obviously everybody in town already knew whose place it was, but pride's precious, and I convinced him all the passing world should see his name. He modestly accepted the notion.

I was about through with the first one when Evvie Ecke came by and stopped, I assumed, to admire my talent.

What she said was, would I come around for dinner that evening?

"I don't think Jennifer would approve," I said with rare honesty.

She smiled. "As a matter of fact, the invitation was her idea. She feels bad about losing her temper with you."

"She told you about that?"

"Oh yes, we have no secrets."

I stopped work and admired the sign, wondering how much of its surface would be paint and how much dust from the graveled road by the time it dried.

Evvie tilted her head and told me I did very fine work. I thanked her. She said if I stayed in town maybe I'd like to do a new sign for Ecke's Drug.

"Going to change the name?" I asked.

"Oh no, we wouldn't do that. Just have a bigger, fresher sign."

"Sort of showing it's under new management, huh?"

She blushed.

"You and Jennifer going to run it together?" I asked.

"Well, probably for a while. We both have ideas and have talked about it some but don't want to do anything too quickly. People might talk."

"Life goes on."

She blushed again. "You're making fun of me. You'll come then, this evening? At six."

"I'll be proud. Will Terry be there?"

"Why not?"

"Just wondered. He wasn't too chummy the last time we talked."

"Don't worry, he'll behave."

I went around to the drugstore when the signs were finished and talked with Elaine. She was wearing a fresh blue-and-white dress that did good things for her, and I let her know it. That got me her big smile.

"I was going to ask you to dinner tonight," I said, "but the surviving Eckes invited me over and I figure I'd ought to go. Could I see you later on?"

She scowled.

"You don't have to feed me to come around."

"Don't be so prickly, I never thought I did. You leery of having your grandma know you're seeing me?"

"I don't neck on the front step, that's all. She's old-timish and it'd upset her."

"So it's okay to come and knock on your door?"

"I sure don't want you throwing sand at my window."

"I'll come around."

"Don't expect too much."

I never expect anything but always hope for the best.

$\triangledown$

21

Pauline answered my knock, greeted me with solemn dignity, and led me into the living room. Jennifer sat on the couch, Terry was on the big corner chair I imagined had been his father's throne, and Baxter was on a couch across from his sister.

The surprise was Jack Springer, parked comfortably on Jennifer's right.

Evvie entered from the kitchen, gave me her hostess smile, and asked me to sit as she took her place on Jennifer's left. Jennifer smiled at me with a look more forgiving than apologetic. Jack was enjoying himself. Terry watched me with his usual sullen stare, and little brother Baxter studied us all with his innocent blue eyes.

I settled into a neutral corner and looked them over.

"I hear you were painting a sign at Durfee's window this afternoon," said Jennifer. "Does that mean Officer Hurlbut knows who the murderer is?"

"Why'd that follow?" I asked.

"Well, until today you were too busy questioning people to do any of your own work, and we heard you were talking with Hurlbut just before lunch. What was that about?"

"He's got his own notions about it."

That didn't please anybody, but before they could start more questions, Pauline, who'd been sitting impatiently in a chair near the kitchen, announced that Jennifer and Jack were engaged.

I fumbled a second before congratulating him, and Evvie

gently told Pauline she should have left that announcement to her sister.

"It didn't seem like she was going to get around to it," said Pauline.

"Some people," Evvie told me, "might think it's too soon after her father's death, but people we care about will understand. She needs support at this time."

"Set a date?" I asked.

"Not yet," said Jennifer. "Probably in October."

"Where'll you live?"

"Not at the Widow Bower's," said Jack and got the laugh he was reaching for.

"They'll live here," said Evvie. "I'm going to buy a house in Aquatown. Pauline and Baxter are coming to stay with me so they can go to school there. Terry's finished high school here and will decide where he wants to go to college."

She looked at her foster family and glowed. All but Terry glowed back. He looked more thoughtful than sullen, and that made me wonder.

"I heard Mr. Ecke's will left everything to Jennifer," I said. "You got money of your own?"

"Everything's been worked out," said Jennifer, gently letting me know the family's financial arrangements were none of my business—which of course I knew.

"Jennifer's very fair," said Evvie. "Basil knew that and that's why he never bothered to change his will."

"You think he might have if he'd known she was going to marry Jack?"

I could have made just as big a hit by letting a fart. Every mouth in the room except Pauline's turned down. Hers popped open in a small o.

Jack worked up a grin.

"I guess you haven't really stopped detecting just because Hurlbut thinks he's got the case solved," he said.

"It was only a question," I said, "not an accusation."

Jennifer sat forward, frowning beautifully.

"Carl, your prejudice is still showing. Daddy wanted the

best for me, but he would never have turned against me because I chose to marry someone he opposed. He just wasn't like that."

"Well," I granted, "you knew him better than I could."

Jennifer gave me her warmest smile and was about to say something when Maude, the hired girl, came to the kitchen door and announced supper.

Evvie rose quickly, thanking her, and started herding us toward the dining room. I felt she was grateful for the maid's timing.

Evvie took the head of the table and sat me on her right. Jennifer sat next to me, Jack across from her, and Terry across from me. Baxter and Pauline faced each other near the foot of the table.

We ate chicken and dumplings with mashed potatoes and gravy. My questions before the serving didn't spoil anybody's appetite; the platters passed swiftly and everyone dug in as if only the first finishers would get dessert.

When Evvie had taken the edge off her appetite, she asked how long I'd be staying in town. I said that'd depend on jobs.

"Are you saying it won't make any difference how you've progressed with Elaine?" asked Jennifer.

"I didn't say anything about that."

"Because you don't care one way or the other?"

"Let's say I feel about that the way you feel about your money matters—it's my business."

That didn't offend her any; she just looked a little smug.

I looked at Evvie. "You got friends in Aquatown? I mean, ones of your own?"

"If you're asking, do I have a potential romance, there are probably more opportunities there than here, but I've none in mind."

I caught a smoldering glare from Terry and ignored it. Evvie noticed too and smiled at him. His face reddened.

"I'm only kidding," she said.

"It's not funny," he said.

"Probably not." Her voice was always gentle with him.

The talk turned general, and soon we had apple pie and drank the last of our coffee. When we returned to the living room, the three youngsters left us. Evvie got comfortable on the couch next to Jennifer and Jack and gave me an arch look.

"I'm sorry to bring up the subject again, but I can't help wondering about your courting Elaine. Do you think she knows something she can tell you about Basil's death?"

"Do you?"

"I can't imagine what."

"Since he seems to have gone after every other woman in sight, I've wondered why she didn't interest him."

"Probably because she was never in awe of him," said Evvie. "Elaine's a simple girl, very conventional. Basil was attracted by slender women, and while he had no scruples about age, I don't think solemn semijuveniles interested him much."

"She seems pretty mature to me," I said.

"Well," said Jennifer with a mocking laugh, "that tells us something about Carl Wilcox, doesn't it?"

"No. It just tells me you don't know her as well as I do."

"Really—you've become that acquainted already?"

"Not *that* acquainted."

They laughed and we talked of other things before I finally asked Evvie if her moving to Aquatown meant she'd give up all interest in the drugstore.

"Well, yes. Once Jennifer and Jack are married, they can handle it. I'll find other interests."

She tried to say it lightly but didn't quite carry it off.

$\triangledown$

22

Eₗₐₛₙₑ'ₛ GRANDMOTHER CAME to the door when I knocked. She was her granddaughter's height, thin, gray-haired, and alert as a blue jay.

"You're not much of a slicker, are you?" she said after looking me over.

"And you're not exactly an old crone."

She grinned, showing good store teeth.

"I've heard about you."

"It's not all true."

"If any of it is, it's scandalous. You look like you had some sense; how'd you manage to get in so much trouble?"

"I wish I could blame it on bad company, but I'm afraid it was mostly booze."

"That's no excuse."

Elaine appeared behind her and gently edged her aside.

"I won't be late," she said.

"I'd hope not. You got to get up early."

We walked slowly along the dark street without talking at first. Crickets gave us a chorus, and somebody laughed on a porch we passed.

"Your grandma's a good-looking woman," I said.

"Everybody says that. Fat lot of good it's done her."

"She have other grandkids?"

She shook her head.

"What happened to her husband?"

"Died in the Civil War. Typhoid in a rebel prison camp."

"So she got a pension?"

She gave me a side look. "You thinking of marrying for money?"

"I don't think she'd have me."

We wound up on the deserted house steps again and sat down. A breeze stirred tree leaves and made fluttering shadows on the berm nearby. Elaine looked at me.

"How long're you going to stay around?"

"Everybody's asking me that today. Why?"

"Like who?"

"The Eckes."

She asked me what they fed me and who was there. She wasn't surprised about Jack Springer.

"I wondered if maybe Mae would be there," she said.

"Why her?"

"She was close to the family before Jennifer's mother died. I mean, close to the kids. She and old Basil never got on."

"So. Did Jennifer ever get together with Mae after the death of her mother?"

"Probably not—I'm not sure. Her father would've been pretty sore, I'd guess."

"You think maybe Jennifer went out to visit her when her old man was out of town?"

She didn't know and was losing interest in the subject, so I tried a switch.

"There was a question about you that came up," I said.

"Yeah? What?"

"How come Basil Ecke never made a pass at you?"

She turned thoughtful and narrowed her eyes.

"Who asked that?"

"I did."

"How'd you know he never did?"

"I didn't. Just thought it'd be interesting to get the reactions from the family. Did you ever wonder?"

"No. I wasn't his type."

"That bother you any?"

"Sure. That's why I went over and broke his nose. Because he snubbed me. Do I write out my confession and give it to you or go straight to Hurlbut?"

"That's what I like about you, you're feisty as hell. Will you break my nose if I kiss you?"

"Try it."

She didn't break my beak, but she bruised my mouth some.

Then she asked what Jennifer's reaction had been to my question.

"She said what you did—not his type. He preferred skinny."

"There was more to it than that. He was already involved with one woman in the store. It would've been pretty awkward messing with two when there were only three employees in the place. If Polly had quit he'd probably have tried me."

"What'd you done if he made a pass?"

"Quit. I didn't need the job that bad and would've been glad for an excuse to leave town."

"To where?"

"Aquatown, Aberdeen, maybe Minneapolis."

"I know a woman runs a hardware store in Aquatown. Maybe she could use you."

"The trouble is, I couldn't leave Grandma."

"Take her along. She's got'a pension."

"She might like it at that."

We started kissing again and she got warm enough I thought we might hit boil, but it never happened, so I walked her home and settled for her hand at the door.

I was walking back to the widow's when Hurlbut came by in his Model A and stopped beside me.

He said it was a nice night. I agreed. He said maybe I'd like to ride with him, he could stand company. I went around and climbed in.

"You don't think one of Bishop's goons did it, do you?" he said as he started through the gears.

"No."

"Baker don't really either. He says the mugs that worked for Bishop wouldn't do it as a favor and he couldn't pay from stir."

He hemmed and hawed a bit before admitting Baker's never been able to believe a hired killer would use anything like a poker for the job.

"He said if they did, they'd beat him to a pulp to be sure."

We drove along a narrow, tree-overgrown lane toward a cemetery and pulled up behind a parked Hudson. After a few seconds under the Model A's lights, a head rose into sight, the engine was started, and the car pulled away.

"That's Johnnie Wilford and Cora Sue Nelson," he told me. "I know the old man's car."

"Why'd you bother?"

"It's no bother. What'd be a bother would be to get out and sneak up on them and make everybody embarrassed. You make them know they can get caught with their pants down any old time, they aren't so likely to get her pregnant. I work it about the same with kids on crab apple raids. Just drive to orchards where they're at it and make a couple passes around while they're on the run. It's exciting for them, and people know I'm awake."

I agreed it was better than having them shot at by a mad orchard owner.

As we drove back toward the commerce street, I said it seemed to me we had to find out what the murder weapon was and check out homes of the more obvious suspects.

"Who you got in mind?"

"Well, we could start with the Widow Bower, the Eckes, the Altmans, and Solomon."

"My God."

"You wouldn't have to ask for a warrant to start. Just see how many of them are willing to cooperate. Remind them it'd be pretty suspicious if they said no."

"My God."

"You've got to try something."

He dithered and said he'd think about it, and I went back to the widow's and probably slept better than he did.

23

HURLBUT SHOWED UP while I was breakfasting with Billie and the Widow Bower. After polite greetings and accepting a cup of coffee, he dug out his pipe, started stoking up, and in a real casual tone asked did she have a poker.

Billie gave him a sharp glance. "You think that'd help you keep that thing lit?"

He actually blushed.

"If you look around," she said, "you'll notice a gas range. You already know there's no fireplace. There's a coal furnace in the basement, and the poker's probably there if you want to check."

"Well now, there's no need to get huffy—"

"We know, Officer Hurlbut, what Mr. Ecke was supposed to have been killed with. You suspect us, don't prance around it, come out and say so."

The widow was slow at picking up on all this, but finally it came to her, and if looks could kill we'd have had a Hurlbut funeral that week.

He gave me an accusing look and explained heavily that he had to check out all possibilities. The widow said go ahead and check. He rose ponderously as a pregnant hippo and went back to the rear vestibule and down the steps.

He came back in a few moments, thanked her, jerked his head at me, and hiked out the front.

"See what that kind of stuff does?" he growled. "Now she's mad at me. That's the way it'll be everywhere I try to check."

"You got a thankless job," I said. "How'd the poker look?"

"Like any other poker. No blood I could see and no dent."

"I can't picture one of those old women swinging a poker hard enough to put a dent in it with Ecke's snoot."

"Hell, neither can I, but I'm only doing what's gotta be done."

"Where next?"

"We'll try the Astors."

"Polly'll be at the drugstore."

"That's all right—we'll more'n likely find her hubby at home. He don't work but a day or two a week, and he's probably sober this early."

He was sober but not awake. It took a lot of knocking and waiting after he hollered hold on, and finally he was at the door, looking sleepy but not particularly hung over, barefooted and wearing wrinkled pants and an undershirt.

"Want to talk with you," said Hurlbut, shoving forward. For a second I thought Julian was going to balk, but then he shrugged and backed inside. We stepped into a hall with a stairway on the right and he led us into the stingy living room. For an awkward moment he stood staring at us, then collapsed onto the couch. We took chairs facing him.

"Where were you Tuesday night?" Hurlbut demanded.

"You asked that Wednesday."

"I'm asking again."

"I was right here."

"Drunk?"

"Mostly."

Hurlbut looked at me. "Why don't you check the kitchen? Julian don't mind, do you?"

Julian looked confused but only shrugged again.

As I moved out, I heard Hurlbut ask how come Julian didn't give a damn when his wife was getting laid by her boss?

The kitchen was neat enough to indicate Polly cleaned it before going to work and her husband hadn't bothered with anything but coffee, which was still warming on the gas range. Down the basement stairs I found the light string and pulled. Near the dark furnace a poker leaned against a metal tub of ashes. It showed no signs of recent violent use.

Back upstairs I opened a couple drawers and poked around. The second one was full of stuff like a can opener, apple corer, and graters. Under a juice squeezer I found a sharpening steel and took it out. It was nearly a foot long and just a tad smaller around than a poker. The handle was hefty, and there was a small metal guard between it and the rod. It opened a whole new vision for me.

I drifted back into the living room where Hurlbut was still ragging Julian, but his heart was no longer in it. He looked up at me. I shrugged. He misunderstood and turned quickly toward Julian.

"Where'd you hide it?" he demanded.

"Behind the flour bin."

That was interesting, so I didn't explain anything to Hurlbut and went back in the kitchen. Opening the flour bin all the way revealed a neat hidey-hole big enough for two quarts of booze. Only one was there.

I went back and told Hurlbut what I'd found.

He gave Julian a sad look, straightened, and climbed to his feet with a painful grunt.

"Okay, Julian, take care."

Julian followed us to the door, where I stopped and turned around.

"What happened in Minneapolis?" I asked.

"Minneapolis?" He looked bewildered.

"What went wrong with the symphony job?"

His mouth sagged. "Who knows?"

"You must."

"No, I don't. That's the trouble."

He closed the door gently.

I guessed the only way he'd settle it was by drinking himself to death.

"I found the poker by the furnace," I told Hurlbut. "It was just like the one you saw at the widow's."

He grunted.

"But I found something interesting in the kitchen," I said. "A sharpening steel."

He jerked his head and looked at me.

"That's a hell of a lot more likely weapon," I said. "It's in kitchens and handy, it doesn't take all that much muscle to handle, and a man might not notice it coming the way he would a thing long as a poker."

He nodded. "All right. You probably got it. When you're back at the widow's, check her kitchen, okay?"

I agreed and asked where we were going now.

"Ecke's."

Just four blocks took us from the small bungalows into the mixed neighborhood of the Widow Bower and Basil Ecke. It's common in small towns to find scrapers next door to those that pile it up.

Pauline was sitting on the porch with Baxter as we approached the house, and they watched us climb the steps and walk toward them. Pauline looked expectant, Baxter was nervous.

Hurlbut greeted them heartily, and they responded politely. "Mrs. Ecke home?" he asked.

"She's in the kitchen with Pearl," said Pauline.

I guessed that was the family cook.

Hurlbut said fine, we'd just go in and chat with her. Pauline frowned her disapproval but said nothing. We went in.

The kitchen was big with a squat coal stove hunkered beside a thin-legged gas range. There was a pump on the right of a white enamel sink and regular plumbing fixtures in the back center. Dark oak cabinets lined two walls. Pearl sat at an enamel-topped table in the center of the room with a cookbook open between her big hands. She had a button nose, lipless mouth, pale gray eyes, gray hair, and matching lashes and brows.

"You're too late for breakfast and too early for lunch," she told Hurlbut. I was ignored.

"How about coffee?" asked Hurlbut.

"Okay," she said, and got up.

Her body was as interesting as her face, but she moved well. She poured for both of us from a big pot on the coal stove, offered cream and sugar, and sat down again.

"You got a sharpening steel?" asked Hurlbut after he tasted the coffee.

"What you want to sharpen?" she asked.

"Nothing. Just want to know if you've got a steel."

She stared at him a second, then nodded toward drawers to the right of the sink. Hurlbut drifted over, set his cup on the counter, and opened the first drawer. It had silver, so he moved to the next. After a little rummaging around he looked at Pearl.

"Is it kept in here?"

"Yes."

"I don't see it."

She gave an exasperated sigh, got up, and pushed him aside. Her rummaging didn't produce it, and with growing irritation she moved to another drawer and finally slammed both shut and muttered something about "that girl."

"You got help in the kitchen?" Hurlbut asked.

"The hired girl—comes in and loses things for me twice a week or more. You like the coffee?"

"It's okay."

"It wouldn't kill you to say thanks. You can't expect midmorning coffee to taste like fresh. Who's the dummy with you?"

Hurlbut grinned and glanced my way.

"Carl Wilcox. He sniffs out murderers, so watch your step."

"I got a lot to worry about in that line. You want a doughnut?" she asked me.

"Be much obliged," I said.

"Well, it can talk—and civil."

She took a round can from the cupboard, removed the top, and set it on the table. It was filled to the brim with plain and powdered doughnuts. They smelled heavenly.

"Where's Mrs. Ecke?" I said, choosing a plain one.

"Went up to her room."

"Where's your room?"

"Above," she said, jerking her chin.

I tried the doughnut and chewed appreciatively before asking if she'd been sleeping up there the night Ecke was killed.

"Why no, I was hobnobbing with the queen of England, where'd you think I'd be?"

"You hear anything in the yard?"

"My man, when I sleep, I die. You work like I do, you sleep sound."

I could imagine the sounds.

"Your doughnuts are great," I told her.

"That mean you want another?"

"Maybe two."

She grinned and shoved the can my way. The grin gave some welcome color to her face. She had good red gums.

Hurlbut appreciated the doughnuts too and asked some questions that got him nowhere as he chewed. Finally I asked if she'd mind letting Mrs. Ecke know we were down here and would like to see her.

She wasn't pleased but went. A moment later Evvie fluttered in, apologizing for not being on hand when we arrived. There was a lot of polite twaddle about that before I managed to bring up the subject of the missing tool. Her eyes opened wide.

"You think that's what killed Basil?"

"Well, something like that'd fit the doc's description of what did it."

She stared at me, then toward Hurlbut.

"We've been checking with everybody," he said hastily. "The Widow Bower, the Astors—and we'll be going on. It's a job got to be done."

Evvie settled into a chair by the kitchen table and accepted a cup of coffee offered by Pearl, who'd followed her in.

"I don't understand, I thought everything was settled—"

"We got to check out everything," said Hurlbut. "It's just routine. You got nothing to worry about."

It was plain she didn't believe him.

"You mind asking Jennifer and the other kids in here?" I asked.

"What for?"

"We got to ask if they know where the steel is," I said.

She looked at Hurlbut apprehensively. He stared back in the dumb misery.

"You want me to round them up?" asked Pearl.

"I guess so."

But Terry wasn't in his room, and we learned from Pauline that Jennifer had gone to Aquatown with Jack.

"They're going to buy an engagement ring!" she told us.

24

Hᴜʀʟʙᴜᴛ ᴡᴀꜱ ʟᴏꜱɪɴɢ steam by then but was too tough to fold and said we'd drive out to Homer's farm and see if he had a steel. I pointed out it was nearly noon, and said that'd mean Homer'd be handy.

Homer was slouched in a chair at the kitchen table when Mae let us in. Like most farm kitchens, it was big and lined with cabinets built so high about a third of the space was beyond the wife's reach. The pump at the sink was their only water source, and a hulking black coal range kept the room cozy in winter and unbearable in summer. Mae had a few sarcastic remarks for Hurlbut and no time for me but offered us lunch. A free meal was almost enough to restore Hurlbut's spirit, and in moments we were chomping sliced pork sandwiches on homemade bread. The coffee was stout, and there was pie for dessert made with green apples and lots of cinnamon.

It was about good enough to make me understand why Homer stayed with his ugly, foul-tempered wife.

She never sat down with us, just hung about, drinking coffee and talking. She said the best thing to happen in the Ecke family over the past fifty-four years was Basil's murder. She said the worst thing was his birth.

"Well," ventured Homer, "he was a good provider and not a bad father."

"Dear God," said Mae, looking heavenward, and then jerked around to refill her coffee cup from the pot on the range.

"So maybe he didn't do so good with Terry," insisted Homer, "but the others turned out fine. You couldn't ask for a finer girl than Jennifer, and everybody loves Pauline. And what's wrong with Baxter?"

"Jen and Pauline can thank their mother for what they are—and the boys their father for what he made them: Terry mean and sullen, Baxter scared sneaky."

"You got a sharpening steel?" Hurlbut asked.

Mae lowered her cup to the counter and stared at him. "What?"

Hurlbut calmly repeated his question.

Mae looked at Homer, who was still chewing his sandwich and didn't look up. She turned back to glower at Hurlbut.

"Why you want a sharpening steel?"

"I just asked did you have one. I didn't ask for it as a gift. You got one or not?"

She looked at Homer again, who was looking at the cop.

"You know what this man's doing?" Mae asked her husband.

He shook his head.

Mae looked back at Hurlbut while still talking to her husband.

"He's accusing us of killing that sonofabitch. Not that I wouldn't like to have. This smartass with him probably dreamed up the notion Ecke was killed with a sharpening steel. Well, Mr. Smartass, we don't own one. So now what're you gonna do?"

"I'd like to look through your drawers," said Hurlbut.

"You mean the ones I'm wearing? Really, Officer!"

Hurlbut turned sunburn red.

"In the cabinets," he said.

"Oh, of course. Well, help yourself, be my guest—"

I looked at Homer. His mouth sagged, his eyes looked bewildered.

Hurlbut, still glowing red, moved to the counter and pulled out the first drawer.

"Jump in, Mr. Smartass," Mae told me. "Help the man out."

"He's just doing his job," I said, "no reason to get sore—"

"You're right. After all, it's no secret I hated the sonofabitch, why not be sure? Hop to it. I'll shut up and leave you to it."

And she clumped out of the kitchen.

We checked all the drawers, went through the cabinets, and found no steel.

Hurlbut apologized to Homer, who sat at the table with his big hands around his coffee cup and only nodded.

A few moments later we climbed into Hurlbut's car and he told me, "No cooking's worth putting up with that woman."

As we were nearing Podunkville I asked if he knew where Alex Solomon lived. He did.

"Let's swing by and talk with his wife."

He shot me a scowling glance.

"What you got in mind?"

"Nothing sure. But we haven't got anything that is, and there was no love lost between Alex and the boss, so maybe we should see if his wife's got any ideas—or a sharpening steel."

He weighed that a few seconds, then grunted and nodded.

The house was a little bigger than I expected, with tall elms on all four corners of a double lot and, for South Dakota at the time, reasonably green grass. We parked out front and strolled up the neat paved sidewalk to an unscreened porch spanning the front.

When Hurlbut knocked, a brown-haired, plump young woman approached down the hall and peered at us through the screen door. A very small boy trotted behind her and pushed against her legs, eyeing us suspiciously.

Hurlbut greeted her warmly and said that was a fine-looking boy there.

She looked down as if surprised to find him and admitted he didn't look too bad. Then she looked at Hurlbut and asked was he going to grill her about the murder?

"Just wanna talk a minute, you don't mind?"

She looked down at her son.

"Okay with you if I talk with Officer Hurlbut?"

The boy moved out of sight behind her wide skirt.

"He doesn't mind," she said and pushed the door open.

We followed her into the living room and sat on furniture I didn't figure came from Montgomery Ward's catalog. The carpet was deep, mostly blue, and covered all but a few inches of hardwood flooring near the walls.

"This is nothing to worry about," he assured her, and I caught a grin that made it clear she considered our visit more of a joke than a threat. Hurlbut plowed on. "You know about Mr. Ecke being killed and we're just checking it out. This is Carl Wilcox, he's from Corden and is helping me some."

Her grin turned my way and broadened, making me think she'd heard stories from her husband that exaggerated everything about me.

"Glad to meet you," she said. "I'm Colleen. And this," she said, looking down at her son who leaned against her knee, "is Patrick."

Patrick turned his back.

"You mind telling us what happened here last Tuesday night?"

"The night Mr. Ecke was murdered?"

Hurlbut nodded.

"We ate supper at our regular time, listened to the radio some, talked about Polly and Mr. Ecke, put Patrick to bed at about eight-thirty, and got him to sleep after nine. About ten we went to bed."

"Alex never left the house?"

"Not even to kill his boss."

"You got a sharpening steel?"

"A what?"

"One of them long things with a handle you run a knife over to give it an edge."

"Oh, sure. We must have one—seems like I've seen Alex use it on Thanksgiving, before he carves the turkey."

"Could we see it?"

She looked back and forth at us.

"What's this about?"

"Just routine, Colleen. You want to get it?"

She wasn't pleased but got up and led us into the kitchen. It was about a third the size of Ecke's and twice as cluttered, with apples, oranges, and peaches in a blue bowl and fresh-picked onions and carrots on the counter near the sink. The walls were lined with white cupboards, and the floor had a checkered black-and-white linoleum floor.

The steel she took from a narrow drawer was shiny and unused looking. Hurlbut gave it a close once-over, handed it back with thanks, and we returned to the living room.

"I'm gonna be honest with you, Colleen," said Hurlbut. "This is a nutsy business and we're getting nowhere. We need all the help we can get. Can you tell us stuff Alex has passed on about work, any little bit that'd help us figure who did this thing?"

"Haven't you asked Alex?"

Hurlbut looked sorrowful. "Come on, you know how touchy he gets if you push him any. All I know is he didn't like the boss and thought probably nobody else did. That doesn't make me think he killed him, but it hints he'd just as soon whoever did it got away with it. Now I'm trying to appeal to you as a responsible woman, a good mother, and my first cousin to give me any help you can."

Colleen bent her head toward the small boy facing her until he lifted his head, and then she smiled. The boy turned his head and gave us a grin I swear looked like he understood everything and was laughing at us.

"All I can tell you," said Colleen, "is you're probably right. I'd help if I could, but the only thing sure is nobody liked Ecke that really knew him. I can't point a finger at anybody and say this one hated him enough to commit murder."

Hurlbut sighed, thanked her, and we left.

"That's a pretty fine house," I said.

"Not bad."

"Nice furnishings."

"Look good."

"It surprises me some a man working for Mr. Ecke'd get pay enough to cover that spread."

Hurlbut grinned.

"Don't let it give you ideas. It happens Colleen's pa was a lawyer who did all right and left her money. Anything else bothering you?"

I had nothing to offer at the moment.

$\triangledown$

25

Hurlbut AND I went back to his office and hashed over the next move. He was for keeping on with the sharpening-steel check and said our best bet was to convince Lt. Baker he should run it in Aquatown going through our whole list of suspects there.

"He won't do it," I said.

"Why not?"

"It'd take too much time. If the killer used a steel, chances are a hundred to one a scared or mad woman did it, grabbing the first thing handy in her kitchen. You're not going to have anybody like Colin Rutledge, Harry Altman, or either of the hotel guys meeting Ecke in a kitchen or smacking him in a panic or snit."

He wrestled that awhile and finally squinted at me.

"So you figure it was in Ecke's place."

"Right where he lived, along with people he'd hit and made mad before. But it could've been in others'."

"Like Polly Astor's or Lola Bishop's or Gloria Altman's."

He scowled some more and started fiddling with his pipe but couldn't work up the effort to light it. The big problem was, neither of us wanted the killer to be a woman.

Hurlbut suggested the killer was a man who used the steel to make it look like a woman did it.

I reminded him he'd decided in the beginning it was me that did it because the body was near where my car had been detired and put on blocks.

"If he wasn't killed at home, somebody had to bring him

back there and set up things so it'd look like I did it. Which would be giving pretty damned mixed signals."

"Well, I suppose when you kill somebody, you don't think real straight right after," he said.

We ran out of gab and thought awhile before I got a notion.

"You know the Eckes' maid?" I asked.

"You mean Maude Shane? She's no maid, she's a hired girl."

"She live in, like Pearl?"

"Naw. Works two, maybe three days a week and comes around when they got a party or something."

"Where's she live?"

"Rooms with the Thompsons on the north side."

I suggested we go talk to her and he said no, he'd call Lt. Baker and see if he'd send a man to check Lola Bishop and the Altmans for sharpening steels. So I got Maude's address and took off.

I remembered her as a small woman with a thin-lipped mouth, tiny, even teeth, and narrow earnest eyes. Behind the screen of the Thompsons' door, which she answered, she looked almost childish.

She remembered me, and when I asked if she could talk a few minutes, she came out and sat on one of three rockers on the front porch while I took one by her side. That left us both facing the street.

I asked general questions at first about her job with the Eckes, how long she'd been with them, how it was working with Pearl, and what did she think of the family. She answered as if everything she said was being written down and might be read by her employers. Pearl was a pearl, Mrs. Ecke was kind, tolerant, and Christian, Jennifer was a perfect lady, and Mr. Ecke had been a perfect gentleman and his loss was a calamity to the family and mankind.

"Were you at the house the day before Mr. Ecke was murdered?"

She nodded. "I do Mondays, Wednesdays, and some weekends, but this time Pearl'd wanted me to do the ironing and some other things on Tuesday, so I went."

"Anything unusual happen?"

"Well, it was all unusual because I don't go Tuesdays usually."

"I mean, did anything seem different with the family. Was anybody upset or nervous, maybe irritable?"

"Oh no," she said so firmly I knew she was lying.

I turned my rocker enough to see her profile, and she lifted her chin a notch to smooth her throat line.

"You know," I said, "that Mr. Ecke was murdered and we're trying to find out why and who did it. It's important you tell the truth and help. People that lie about a murder got a good chance to share the blame—you know that?"

"I don't see how," she said without looking at me.

"Believe me. It's called being an accessory. By lying about a murder or any of the facts connected, you help the killer get away with it, and that's against the law."

She thought about that and glanced at me.

"I haven't lied."

"Come on, Maude, if I swallowed all you told me, it'd been impossible for a murder to happen at Ecke's. You're telling me Basil Ecke was a plaster saint and all the family was pure as Christ. If that was so, the man'd be alive and well, not dead and buried. Now I think he was sore as a boil and something was building up. What was it?"

She squeezed her thin lips tight, took a deep breath, leaned slowly back against the chair, and for a long moment sat with her eyes closed. Finally they opened.

"All right," she confessed, "I guess Mr. Ecke was upset."

"About what?"

"I don't know for sure—but it was plain he was good and mad when he came back from Aquatown Monday night. I heard him talking in the living room to Mrs. Ecke or Jennifer—I don't know which because I didn't see either of them, only heard voices real low in there. I could see Pearl was upset too. She was cross as a bear with me before I went home. Mr. Ecke was off to the store when I came Tuesday morning, but he showed up early that afternoon, which was something I never knew him to do before. I'd finished the ironing and was helping Pearl pickle peaches in the kitchen. She makes grand pickled peaches—well—anyway, I stayed on to help serve dinner and Jennifer didn't show and Terry looked scared and poor Baxter was bug-eyed and shivery. Mrs. Ecke just didn't look herself at all."

"Where was Jennifer supposed to be?"

"I don't know. Pearl never tells me anything about family, and I dassn't ask questions, she'd take my head off."

"How late did you stay at the house?"

"Till after supper. Pearl and I ate in the kitchen, and I'd just finished when Mrs. Ecke came out and said I could go home now, it was late and I'd had a long day. She never done anything like that before. I offered to help do dishes, but she shooed me out saying it was late. It was plain she wanted to get rid of me. And she told Pearl to go to bed. You should've seen old Pearl's face. She was fit to be tied. So we left the kitchen all a mess."

We sat still a few moments while a robin sang in a nearby elm.

I asked if she knew what a sharpening steel was.

"It's that thing sort of like a dagger with no point."

"Was there one on the counter when you left the kitchen?"

She frowned. "Could've been—most everything else was, and Pearl used it on the carving knife before she cut the roast. Why?"

"It could be important. Did Jennifer get home before you left?"

"No. There was some telephoning back and forth and I think maybe hers was one of the calls, but she wasn't home yet when I left."

"You know her aunt Mae?"

She glanced at me.

"Yes."

"She ever come around the Eckes' house?"

"Oh no. Mr. Ecke couldn't stand her."

"How'd you know that if nobody in the house ever told you anything?"

"Well, that's a thing everybody in town knows. They've always known that."

"You know if Jennifer ever went to visit her aunt?"

"Well, I wouldn't know anything about that."

"You never heard she did?"

"I might have. She wouldn't tell Mr. Ecke if she did."

I thanked her, said I'd do my best to see she didn't get in trouble talking to me, and left.

$\triangledown$

26

BACK AT HURLBUT'S office I found him jawing with a local citizen. When it began to look as if that'd go on till fall, I headed over to the drugstore. Elaine was busy with a customer, but Polly came up to ask if she could help. At our first meeting all I noticed was her height and the wide, sad mouth. Now I took in the pale, smooth skin over her face and throat and the small wrinkles at the corners of her clear blue eyes.

"If the offer's genuine, yeah."

That rattled her enough to make me feel like a heel, and I said what I really wanted was a favor she had no reason to offer.

"I don't understand," she said apologetically. She was a woman always on the defensive.

"You remember seeing me with Officer Hurlbut?" I asked.

"Yes."

"Okay, so I'm working on that business. Now, you were close to Mr. Ecke and he must've talked to you a lot. Did he tell you if his daughter Jennifer was friendly with her aunt Mae?"

Her look darted to Elaine and her customer, back toward Solomon's counter, and finally around to me once more.

"Why do you ask?"

"Why don't you answer?"

"Well, it hardly seems, I mean—"

"In a case like this, everything's important. There're no real leads and we're digging. That means all kind of questions that should be nobody's business have to be answered. You've got to remember you and your husband are suspects in this thing, and it can help your case if you can help us."

It cost her some but she finally answered.

"All I know is Basil hated Mae and wouldn't have her in his house and I'm sure didn't want his daughter having anything to do with her. She—Mae—said Basil murdered Olivia—it's not surprising he'd be mad. And he was certain she'd try to alienate his children if she could get close, so he did everything he could to make them stay away from her."

"You ever hear about the incest rumors?"

"Of course. Basil was convinced Mae started them, probably in cahoots with Billie."

"They were friends?"

"Oh yes, for years, and they had a common cause. They both hated Basil."

I asked if Basil talked about his son Terry.

That bothered her enough so she stopped meeting my eyes for a moment.

"I don't understand what you're after."

"Did he have plans for him, where he wanted him to go to college, whether he thought he'd ever make out in school?"

"He was very uncomfortable about Terry. He's a difficult boy. I know he planned for him to attend college, one of the Ivy League schools, I believe, but he wasn't sure he'd be accepted. Terry isn't a great student."

"Was he obedient?"

"He tried to give that impression, but Basil didn't trust him. As a matter of fact, he told me Terry was in love with Evvie—and that she encouraged him in subtle ways to get back at Basil for his interest in me."

The last of that came out in a whisper.

I decided she needed a letup and asked how long Pearl had worked for the family. She thought a moment and said it must be nearly twenty years.

"So she knew the first Mrs. Ecke well?"

"Very. I believe they were even classmates long ago."

"What'd Pearl think of Ecke?"

"Well, it was a prickly relationship. Basil admitted he was totally dependent on her in the home, but he got very exasperated at times, just as he did with Alex here in the store. Pearl and Alex are both very contrary, irritating, and sarcastic."

"You think Pearl believed he killed his first wife?"

"Oh, I doubt that—although Basil did tell me she implied it more than once—but he thought it was just her need to be snotty because deep down she resented being a menial. That's what he thought made her that way. Resentment. She worked it off by showing she didn't think her boss was really superior."

"Ecke said that?"

"Uh-huh."

"He talked to you a lot?"

"Oh yes." She smiled with a sad fondness. "He was a fascinating talker—I've never known his equal. Always thinking and studying people, figuring them all out. Like, he told me Evvie married him because she wanted children but didn't want to give birth."

"What'd he say about his first wife?"

The smile vanished. "He didn't talk about her."

"You ever wonder about that?"

"I understood. I don't believe for a second he killed her, but he felt guilty because he'd hit her when they were married. He was very ashamed of his temper. It was a curse."

"Didn't he get mad at you?"

"No. Never. I never gave him cause."

"You ever wonder why he kept Evvie if he wasn't satisfied with her?"

"No. He told me. She was good for the children and they loved her. And she was content with that."

"So why'd he hit her?"

"She made him feel guilty, I guess."

Two ladies came in the front door, so Polly said I'd have to excuse her and went to greet them. By this time Elaine's customer had left and I joined her.

"Can I take you to dinner tonight?" I asked.

"Why don't you come over to Grandma's?" she said.

"You think Grandma'll let me in?"

"It's her idea. But she won't go to bed and leave us alone on the couch."

I said I'd come around. She told me to make it six sharp.

27

HURLBUT TOLD ME Lt. Baker had agreed to have one of his men check out the Altman and Bishop kitchens if the parties concerned cooperated. He wasn't about to try to get a search warrant. Being a worrier, Hurlbut figured that meant we probably wouldn't get the help needed. I told him not to sweat, I'd make another trip if Baker flopped.

Elaine let me into her grandmother's house at six. The front door opened directly on the living room just big enough for a daybed, an easy chair, and a small round table surrounded by two straight-backed chairs and a folding job with a sagging cloth seat. I guessed when there was no company the folding job was stored in the basement. The table had a white cover, the dishes were blue and white, and the silver plate looked well worn.

I guessed Elaine slept on the daybed and her grandmother had the bedroom off the northwest corner.

Grandma came from the kitchen to meet me and was so tiny she made me feel big as a heavyweight fighter. She didn't offer to shake hands. When I thanked her for the invitation, she said if Elaine was bound to keep seeing me, she felt obliged to get acquainted.

I told her the house smelled wonderful. She said it could be her Evening in Paris perfume or maybe it was the meat loaf in the oven.

"It's nothing special, but we'll have corn on the cob with it, which I suppose you'll like. Most men do."

After she said grace and we started eating, she asked where

I'd gone to school. I said in Corden.

"Graduate?" she asked.

"Afraid not."

"I suppose you got kicked out."

"Your supposer is in good shape."

"How'd you manage to travel so?"

"I've got a hand for portable jobs."

"What you've done is, you've bummed about, that's what it comes to, right?"

"You got it."

"And with all your travels, you've come down to thinking South Dakota's beautiful. Have you really convinced yourself of that?"

"I don't figure it's a comedown."

That got me a scornful look from the old lady and a sympathetic grin from Elaine.

The meat loaf was tolerable when I added enough salt, the corn was sweet, and later on she served great brownies that were rich, heavy, and unfrosted.

I asked what she'd heard of the Ecke family.

"You like gossip?"

"Yup."

She grinned, and I could see Elaine in it. An accepting, inviting look, honest and bold.

"All right," she said. "You tell me what you've heard and I'll tell you what you've missed."

So I went into the wife beatings, the woman chasing, the tales of incest and possible murder. She took it all in, nodding now and again.

When I was through, she allowed I'd managed to pick up all the common gossip. Then she said that in her opinion, Ecke's biggest problem was he didn't really like women but needed them so bad he was all appetite, so he kept going from one to another looking for one that could settle the hunger.

"Of course, if he'd found one he'd probably've killed her. And I don't mean the way he did Olivia—that was more than likely an accident—he wasn't passionate enough about her for

killing. He wanted to be a king—was certain that's what he
was born for—nobody was good enough to be on his level. He
knew more about anything that interested him than anybody
else, and anything he didn't know more about was beneath
contempt. One reason he hated Mae was she was onto him
and smart as him. Way back, when Homer was first married
to her, they were together all the time—Olivia, Mae, Homer,
and Basil. At first they had fun fighting and then it got serious
and finally they just couldn't stand the sight of each other."

She sipped coffee, thought a moment, and went on.

"What really cinched it was, Mae started getting close to
Jennifer when the girl was still real young. It gave Basil the
horrors. He was convinced Mae'd turn her against him.
Because the fact is, Jennifer's the only female Basil ever truly
loved—"

"How can you know this?" I asked.

She gave a laugh that was like a snort.

"I don't really know it—but what I'm telling you came
from Mae, and like I said, she's smart and I imagine she had
it right."

"You, Billie Fielding, and Mae are buddies, right?"

"Along with Fannie Bower," she nodded.

"When'd you all meet last?"

"The Sunday before Basil Ecke got killed."

"Where?"

"At Fannie Bower's. We been meeting there Sundays for
fifteen years."

I stared at her for a few seconds and finally asked, "Was
Jennifer there?"

She smiled. "Why'd she be there when her daddy'd not
approve?"

"Her daddy was in Aquatown. She came over to see Mae."

"Well, aren't you clever? What you suppose she wanted to
see Mae about?"

"I think her dear daddy had told her he was cutting her
out of his will if she married Jack. She wanted to talk it over
with Mae because Mae was the smartest woman she knew."

"You want some more coffee?" she asked. The smile was gone.

I said sure. Elaine waved her down and went after the pot.

"I don't know what Jennifer wanted to talk about," said the old woman. "They went into the living room and I stayed with Fannie and Billie in the kitchen."

"But you heard later."

"No," she said positively. "They were still at it when I left the back way so's not to bother them."

"Uh-huh. And you've never talked to Mae since?"

"No."

"How does Mae get to your Sunday meetings?"

"Drives in their car. Got a Chevy."

"And she didn't come around this last Sunday?"

"That's right."

We looked at each other awhile, and finally Elaine started clearing the table. I got up and helped. The old lady finished her coffee and watched us. She worked up a smile once more.

"You surprise me," she said when Elaine began filling a pan in the sink with soapy water and I helped myself to a dish towel from a hanger on the wall.

"How?" I asked.

"I'd not expect a hobo to help with dishes. But that's nowhere near as strange as you getting involved with a murder. What's it to you?"

"I got into it because somebody set me up to take the rap. That makes me sore, since for some reason cops always like me as the number-one suspect anyway."

"But you aren't anymore."

I granted that.

"You getting paid?"

"No."

"So forget it. Nobody wants to know who did this but old Hurlbut, and he's paid to worry about such stuff but not enough to let it drive him crazy. And you don't really know somebody tried to make it look like you were the killer. It was just circumstances, more than likely."

"Well, Grandma," I said, "the reason I was never a success as a bum is I always hated leaving a job not done. And I got to know the real reason this guy died."

"What you're saying is, you're nosy."

"That's how it is with us homely philosophers."

I handed her that opening free, but she tossed it.

She got to her feet easy as a girl, moved over to Elaine, and touched her shoulder.

"I'm going for a walk. Just keep in mind I'll be back any time at all so don't embarrass me when I come in, all right?"

Elaine told her to go ahead.

When we were alone, I asked how she thought her grandmother'd liked me.

"Pretty good."

I'd thought I was doing fine up until she tried to talk me out of following up on the murder. Then the whole tune changed.

"But she wants me to butt out."

She didn't deny it. We finished the dishes without more gab and sat down on the daybed.

"When do you really think she'll be back?" I asked.

"It'll be a while. And when she does come, she won't sneak in trying to catch us."

So I kissed her and she kissed back, and we got quite a bit more involved than before. I was surprised how large and hard her nipples got, and when I tried checking further she said no, nothing was going to go on below the waist.

I told her quite a bit was starting there for me, and she said she understood that was pretty normal.

"How much do you really know?" I asked.

"Not much. And I'm not going to learn tonight."

So I did the best I could with what was offered and her reaction raised my hopes to the aching area, but finally she gave a great sigh and said whoa. I don't know if she was any more surprised than I was when I backed off.

She buttoned up, straightened her clothes, and sat straight.

"I guess you're going to have this thing solved pretty quick," she said.

"Which thing?"

"The murder."

"Oh. Well, maybe."

"Where'll you go when you leave town?"

"Maybe west."

"How about Minneapolis?"

"That where you want to go?"

"Yes."

"And you want me to give you a ride?"

"Uh-huh. I'll pay for the gas."

"Then what?"

"I won't put out."

"I didn't think you would."

"Will you do it?"

"Why not?"

"I don't want you to think I've just been leading you on. I like you an awful lot. I've got to get out of this town. I'm afraid to go alone and I trust you—which may seem dumb, but the way you've been I just believe in you. You think we could leave tomorrow?"

"You'd quit your job without notice?"

She leaned against my shoulder, lowering her head.

"I suppose not. But I'd like to. How soon can we go?"

"When it's over and I make a little more money painting signs."

"I can loan you a little."

I tipped her head back.

"What's going on? You think your grandma clobbered old Ecke?"

She shook her head. "But it had to be somebody I know—and I don't want any of them sent to prison."

"From all I've heard, if we nail the killer, whoever it is will probably get off on a justifiable-homicide claim."

"I wish I could believe that."

$\triangledown$

28

Bud ELLIOT HAD been waiting in his secondhand Buick not half a block down the street. He came out of the front seat nice and easy, and I caught sight of the baseball bat he was trying to hide behind his right leg as he walked to meet me. It didn't seem likely he'd be alone, so I looked around quick and sure enough, on my left, there was Pinky slipping past the corner of the nearest house. He wasn't bare-handed either.

I took off across the street. They came pounding after.

As I raced across an alley, I glanced back and saw Bud was gaining. I cut right at the rear of a bungalow and on reaching the next corner spied Pinky coming hard. The baseball bats didn't slow either of them.

What the hell, they were both younger than me and could probably run twice as long. I picked a good box elder with low limbs, jumped for one, caught hold, swung my legs up and over, and the next second was going up the next limb. I didn't stop until I was in the center of thick brush, looking down at them. They stood a moment, puffing and searching the round for rocks. There was only grass, weeds, and bare earth.

"Come on up," I suggested. "The view's great."

Bud moved until he was almost directly below me.

"All you got to do," he said so quietly I could barely hear, "is climb down, go get your stuff from the Widow Bower's, get in your tin lizzie, and take off."

"No. Hurlbut wouldn't like it. I wouldn't like it."

"If we got to come and get you, your own mother wouldn't recognize what we'll haul out of town before light."

"You come and get me, sonny boy, and you may never see light."

"Let's get him," growled Pinky.

I thought some of starting to holler but had trouble accepting the notion of a crowd gathering to see me treed by a couple punks. They muttered to each other a few seconds, then Bud handed his bat to Pinky and reached for the first branch. He was strong enough, but awkward, and I took what satisfaction that gave me. When he was perched he took his bat back, grabbed Pinky's, and a moment later they were both in the tree. They tried to work up together on opposite sides of the main trunk and had trouble trying to hang on to their weapons. They were about ten feet up when Pinky's bat slipped out of his hand, smacked against a lower branch, and went skittering on the lawn.

There was some cussing and more talk, and they started up once more. Pinky moved a little faster without the bat, and I was happy to see it. When he was pretty close, I dropped toward him, caught a stout limb four feet over his head, and slammed into his chest with both knees. He screamed and was gone. I pulled myself back up and invited Bud to hurry.

I expected he'd worry about his friend, but the yell only made him mad, and he came swarming after me. When he swung his bat, I ducked behind the trunk, which he punished something awful at the expense of his own hand. While he was trying to regroup, I swung around the trunk and caught him with my foot right on the collar line.

And then there were none.

I climbed down, checked the damage, and went after Hurlbut.

29

Doc Penzler said Pinky's ribs were severely bruised and his right femur was fractured. Bud had a sprained ankle and a fractured collarbone.

"Aside from those little details, some pretty nasty bruises, and a total loss of humor, they came out well considering the fall. I take it you sustained no injuries?"

"Scraped my left hand on the bark somewhere along the line," I said.

He looked at it and told me I'd survive.

Hurlbut questioned the two guys separately. Pinky was hardly willing to admit his name. Bud was almost as cooperative. After a while I asked Hurlbut if he'd let me talk with him in private a few minutes. He got pretty worried about that, but I promised him faithfully I'd not lay a hand on the dear lad and he could stand right outside the door to come a-running if he heard a squeak. So he went off.

"If I press charges," I told Bud, "you could take the rap for assault with a deadly weapon and attempted murder. Now dammit, you're not dumb enough to take that. Tell me who put you up to this and I'll tell Hurlbut I'm not signing any complaint, and the worst you could get is a trespassing charge if the owner of that tree bitches about busted limbs."

"Why the hell'd anybody have to put me up to it? You were messing with my gal."

"What the hell brought you to Podunkville on a weeknight when you got to be up before dawn on your job? You knew I was seeing Elaine but didn't come running with a ball bat before. I think somebody told you she was planning to run off with me. Just tell me if that's so and who called."

He stared at me, blinked, and looked at the ceiling.

"All right. I heard you were taking her off. Was that right?"

"She asked me for a ride to Minneapolis. Elaine's not putting out to me and isn't planning marriage. She just wants out of town and on her own. She offered to pay for gas."

"What's she want away from?"

"Maybe she's tired of Pinky spying on her and you acting like you own her. But more likely she wants something better than working in the drugstore and living in Podunkville."

"I asked her to come to Aquatown."

"Where you'd still act like you owned her."

"I ain't that bad."

"You ain't that good, either. Not now. You both got lots of time."

"Not me. She's gonna think I'm a damned fool. Everybody will."

"Well, don't prove it by being bullheaded. Who called you? Was it Elaine's grandma?"

"It was Pinky. He got the call. So right away he called me at the boardinghouse and I came and got him and we waited for you."

"The bats were his idea, I'd guess."

"Yeah. We weren't really gonna pound you—just scare you good and make you take off. When you went up that tree, I didn't know what the hell to do but couldn't leave it at that. And when you knocked Pinky off I went a little nuts."

"Pinky know who called him?"

"Naw, he got all excited and didn't ask. And if he knew he wouldn't tell you no matter what."

"Not even if you asked him to?"

"I wouldn't ask him. I couldn't do a thing like that."

Hurlbut poked his nose in, and I didn't object.

"You get anyplace?"

"Somebody called Pinky and told him Elaine and I were getting ready to run off to Minneapolis."

"Who?" Hurlbut demanded, looking at Bud.

"He doesn't know," I said.

"Look," Hurlbut told Bud, "we're investigating a god-damned murder. You attacked this man and I know damned well it wasn't just over a piece of fluff. Somebody thinks he's gettin' too close and wants him stopped. Well, I'm in this too, and by God this is gonna get settled."

He shouldn't have called Elaine a piece of fluff or made light of Bud's great romance. He clammed up and wouldn't even admit he'd told me about the call to Pinky.

By the time we got back to City Hall, I was tired of the whole business, and after agreeing to talk with Grandma Fitzgerald in the morning, I headed back to the widow's and the sack.

30

THE WIDOW BOWER was alone and reserved when I came down in the morning. She seemed uneasy as she greeted me without meeting my eyes and filled the cup at my place.

"Where's the gang?" I asked.

"Billie's not feeling well," she said, placing the coffeepot back on the range, "and Jack's out of town."

"Are you telling me he stayed overnight in Aquatown with Jennifer?"

She looked at me with stern disapproval. "Well, it's all quite proper—Jennifer's staying with her cousin and Jack's at his friend's house."

"They've made the trip an overnighter before?"

"I didn't say that—"

"I guess Jack told you their plans, huh?"

She faced me squarely, hands on hips.

"You want fried eggs with your bacon?"

"That'd be fine. Over easy."

She turned back to the stove.

I let the silence hang as the bacon started sizzling and finally said I'd heard she hostessed a little Sunday coffee party for ladies every week in this kitchen.

"Most weeks," she admitted as she turned the bacon.

"Not this last one?"

"No. It didn't seem right under the circumstances."

"Where's your telephone?"

She turned from the skillet and stared at me a second before answering. "It's in the hall, under the stairs. You planning to make a call?"

"I might have to. Did Elaine's grandma use it last night?"

Her head jerked, and she threw me an angry look.

"Why'd she use my telephone?"

"She hasn't got one of her own. Did she use it?"

She looked me in the eye.

"No sir, she absolutely, positively did not use my telephone."

"Oh. She just asked you to make the call?"

"I don't know what you're talking about," she said, jabbing at the innocent bacon.

"Mrs. Bower, I know she was here last night."

The widow was too honest to realize I was only guessing. She turned casual. "Well, yes, she did drop by. If you must know, she thought it'd be kind if she left you and Elaine alone for a bit. She understands things like that and trusts Elaine."

"And she and you, Mae, and Billie are all great pals and don't want anybody to find out who killed Ecke, right?"

She calmly removed the bacon from the frying pan, poured out some of the grease, and broke two eggs into the skillet.

"What a strange thing to say. Why'd we not want that?"

"Because all of you hated him, and maybe one of you killed him. If it wasn't one of you, it was Jennifer or Evvie. But whoever it was, you ladies figured it was strictly a proper murder and ought to be unsolved."

She calmly splashed grease over the eggs and shook her head. "You've quite an imagination."

"If it was self-defense," I said, "whoever did it could get off, you know. That's how I figured it. Old Ecke lost his temper once too often, and he did it in a kitchen where the woman he was bullying had a sharpening steel at hand. She just grabbed it and swung on him. The only thing that bothers me is that whoever did it, or her friends, tried to hang a frame on me."

She turned the two eggs smoothly, put the bacon on a plate, moved it next to the skillet, and deliberately moved the eggs over and brought them to me. As I salted and peppered them, she delivered freshly buttered toast and sat down across from me.

"I think you've got that figured wrong. Doing your car was all Terry's idea—he's like that. He wasn't crazy about his father, but he *was* his father and he couldn't let some bandy-legged stranger come around and hand him sass. So he showed you. That's all there was to it."

"And the body would've been dumped out there, no matter, huh?"

"Probably."

"And the telephone call to Pinky had nothing to do with the murder—Grandma Fitzgerald just wanted to have me run out of town and knew Bud would come to do it."

"Something like that. Did they really have ball bats?"

"Yes."

"Well, I'm sure that was just for show. They were trying to scare you, and it must've worked if you ran up a tree."

"I didn't run up, I climbed. What you call a strategic retreat."

"And they both fell out of it?"

"They got some help."

"You do take pride in being a roughneck, don't you?"

"It's about all I got going for me," I admitted.

She gave me a smile, and I don't think it hurt her a bit.

"Well, I'm glad we had a chance for this little chat. Now you understand things better. How soon will you be leaving?"

"Pretty soon, I think."

"I hope you don't plan to take Elaine."

"That's up to her."

"It'd be awful hard on her grandmother. Give that some thought."

"I figure she'll make out, long as she's got you and the rest of the coffee crowd."

She smiled again, but it didn't look too happy.

"I'm afraid," she said, "it'd been better if you'd never come to town."

"I'm about convinced you're right."

31

IT WAS NEAR 10:00 A.M. when I got to the drugstore. There were no customers. Alex, Polly, and Elaine were together by the back counter and watched me approach. Alex was thoughtful, Polly apprehensive. Elaine's expression stumped me. It looked defiant, as if she expected a fight she wasn't eager for but wouldn't duck.

"Can you spare Elaine a few minutes?" I asked Alex.

"Well," he said, "as you can see, we're pretty swamped right now, but—?"

Elaine walked at my side to the street, and I steered her south.

"Did you tell your grandma you were going to ask me to drive you to Minneapolis?"

"Of course."

"Whose idea was it, really, to invite me over?"

"We just agreed on it."

"Was the real reason because you two wanted to talk me out of trying to find Ecke's killer?"

"That was Grandma's reason. Mine was, I wanted a ride to Minneapolis and I wanted you to take me."

I considered that.

"Don't you believe me?" she asked.

"Yeah, I guess I do."

"You say that like it surprised you."

"Everybody else in town has lied to me—I'm so used to it a straight story sounds funny."

"Well, I'd like it if you didn't mess with the murder. But

I won't be mad if you stay with it. And I didn't know Bud and Pinky were going to try and run you off."

"Did your grandma tell you?"

"Not till after. She still won't believe they were going to use ball bats on you. She's got herself convinced of that."

"You know what happened?"

"They chased you up a tree and you knocked them both off. Everybody knows that."

"Is anybody connecting this with the murder?"

She stopped and faced me, squinting against the bright sun.

"You think it was?"

"Oh yeah."

"You think I was involved?"

"You don't have a sharpening steel in your kitchen."

"Is that why you helped with dishes, to check?"

"It wasn't the only reason."

She suddenly got self-conscious and looked around the street. Only an old couple and a young boy were in sight, but all three were watching us.

She took my arm and began walking.

"When I go," I said, "if you still want along, I'll take you."

She stopped again and tugged my arm till we were facing each other.

"You mean it?"

I nodded.

"How soon?"

"I'd guess less than a week."

She drew back a fraction.

"That means you're not quitting the murder."

"I haven't made any conditions; you can't either, or it's no deal."

She stared at me a moment. "All right. Fair enough. I'll give notice when I get back. As of Saturday, I'm through."

"Sure you don't want to talk with Grandma first?"

"You come with me when I do. I told her I'd be home for lunch and bring you if you'd come."

I had to laugh and she did too.

"You really got me figured, haven't you?" I said.

"I didn't tell her it was sure, I just hoped. She warned me you'd be fed up and never speak to me again—but I figured you'd give me a chance to explain and it'd be okay."

We agreed I'd walk her home at noon, and she went back to the drugstore. I went to talk with Doc Penzler.

He was in his office reading a medical journal and grinned broadly when his nurse sent me in.

"Well, have you discovered you need attention to damages suffered last night?" he asked.

"Nope, no problems in that line. How're Bud and Pinky doing?"

"It's fascinating. With the exception of Pinky's broken leg, the most severe damages to both those men were inflicted by you. The knees to Pinky's ribs and the kick to the collarbone of Bud. I think your hands and feet might be classified as deadly weapons."

"What I want to know is, if we find the sharpening steel, could you tell if any blood on it was human?"

"Me? No. But there might be scientists in the East who could. Doctor Karl Landsteiner got the 1930 Nobel Prize in physiology for classifying human blood types, and I've heard that could be helpful in forensic medicine. You could check with your police lieutenant in Aquatown to see if he's heard of such procedures."

I thanked him and, after some more gab, set off to pick up Elaine.

Just before I reached the door, Jack Springer drove by with Jennifer in his Model A. Neither of them noticed me, and the car turned south, heading for the Ecke place.

Elaine met me inside and we headed for her home.

Grandma Fitzgerald served egg salad sandwiches, I suspected because eggs were selling for eleven cents a dozen those days, and while that's low on my list of favorites, I managed to wash it down with her good coffee. We had sugar cookies for dessert.

She was only moderately apologetic about setting up my fracas with Bud and Pinky and gently chastised me for getting so rough with a couple young boys who actually meant no harm. She also let us both know she disapproved strongly of our traveling so far together, but she assured Elaine she trusted her and would assume all would go well.

And she insisted on assuming we were going to leave in the next day or so despite Elaine's clear announcement that she intended to finish out her week at the drugstore.

"What're you going to do now?" Elaine asked as we walked back toward the drugstore.

"Go over and talk with Jennifer. I've never been able to ask if she knows what happened to the family sharpening steel."

"You think she did it, don't you?"

"I think that's what everybody wants me to guess."

"Why'd they do that?"

"Because she'd be the hardest for anybody to bring a case against. She's young, a knockout, engaged. . . . You couldn't convict her with any South Dakota jury you could find."

"So why try?"

"I won't. But I still want to know what happened."

She shook her head. "You're a case, Carl Wilcox. A nut."

It was a hard point to argue.

▽

32

PAULINE GREETED ME at the Eckes' front door and when I asked for Jennifer said she wasn't home.

"That's funny, I just saw her on Main Street in Jack Springer's car a few minutes ago."

Pauline shrugged. "They didn't come here."

"Okay, is Evvie home?"

She said yes, invited me into the living room, and went after her stepmother. Evvie appeared a few moments later, looking tired. I apologized for bothering her, told her about seeing Jennifer with Jack Springer a while earlier, and asked if she'd any idea where they might have gone.

"Probably out to Mae's," she said.

"Ah. Was she out there the night her father got murdered?"

She stared at me a moment before answering.

"I don't know where she was that night, Carl. All I know is, she wasn't home."

"She told me she was."

"She wasn't. That's why her father was so angry when he left the house. He'd been up to her room and found she was gone when he'd told her to stay in."

"So he was headed for Homer's farm, right?"

"He may have been."

"I suppose it was Terry that told him where she'd gone."

She actually looked surprised.

"Why'd he do that?"

"Because he was jealous of Jennifer and hoped Basil'd

make good on a threat to disown her and leave his money to you."

She looked down at her hands, then into space, and finally back to me.

"I guess you could be right. I suspected more than once Terry hated his sister. Despite everything, he had a great admiration for his father and wanted his approval desperately. And he was so sick of Jennifer being the worshiped one."

"Where's Terry now?"

"In his room, listening to the radio."

I thought quite a while before asking her my next question.

"Would you ask him to come down and tell me the truth about what happened that Tuesday night?"

"I'd rather not."

"Yeah, I don't blame you. But keep in mind, if Jennifer killed him and Terry'd tell the truth, the will Basil hadn't changed yet would be no good and that'd leave you the works."

She gave me a haggard look and lowered her head.

"I wouldn't want to get it that way."

"Okay. You're all right, Evvie. But I'm going up to talk with Terry if you don't mind."

"I can't stop you."

"Just say no."

"Don't put it on me."

"Good enough."

I went up the stairs and tapped on the first bedroom door. Baxter opened it and started at the sight of me.

"Your brother's room the next on this side?" I asked.

He nodded.

I moved to the next door and tapped.

"Yeah?"

"Wilcox," I said. "I want to talk with you."

A couple seconds passed and then the door opened. He turned his back on me and went back to the bed, flopped down, and stretched out.

I found a chair shoved under a cluttered desk, pulled it
out, and parked on it backwards, resting my forearms over
the back.

"You've had a damned tough time, haven't you?"

I thought the approach surprised him, but after a moment
he said, "Whaddaya want?"

"When did your dad tell you he was cutting Jennifer out
of his will?"

He brought his arms up, laced his fingers behind his head,
and stared at the ceiling.

"Where'd you hear that crap?"

"Not from Evvie. She wouldn't tell me a thing about you.
But it figures. Somebody told your dad Jennifer was visiting
Mae and it had to be you from all I've seen and heard so far.
You told him because you're in love with Evvie and want her
to get his money, not Jennifer, who turned against him,
getting all friendly with your aunt who claims your pa killed
your mother."

"That's more crap."

"You thought a lot of your father, didn't you?"

He didn't answer.

"You were mad at me when I got smart with him. That's
why you took the wheels off my crate—not because he asked
you to but because you knew he'd get a kick out of you
showing me up after I nastied him. And you felt for him
because he was all shook up about your sister double-crossing
him, and since then you've been thinking it's your fault he
went charging out to the farm crazy mad so Jennifer killed
him to stop him from beating her up."

"I don't believe Jennifer did it. It was that Jack Springer
sonofabitch."

"Why'd you hide the sharpening steel?"

"I didn't."

"Who did?"

"How'd I know? Maybe Jen thought that'd make you
dummies think he was killed here and then you'd suspect
Evvie and me along with the rest."

That was just what I'd figured, so naturally I got a new respect for the kid's brain.

"You're not dumb at all, are you?"

"I know a few things."

"Yah, like you knew Jack was with Jennifer at Mae's place, and you tipped off your old man, who went out and got killed, and now Evvie'll be able to buy a new house in Aquatown."

He sat up and put his feet on the floor.

"You don't know anything's going to do you any good. Why don't you just hit the road?"

"Sooner or later, I will," I said, getting up. "So long."

▽

33

It took a little while, and Hurlbut wasn't totally convinced of my theory even when he agreed to drive out to Homer Ecke's farm. There was a little delay in getting the search warrant, but finally we had it in hand and wheeled across the rolling prairie southwest.

Jack Springer's dusty Model A stood in the front yard, and Mae appeared behind the screen of the side door as we approached.

Hurlbut asked if Jennifer was inside.

"What if she is?"

"Got a question to ask."

Mae turned and called. We reached the stoop and stopped. A moment later Jennifer was at Mae's side.

"Yes?"

"You know what happened to the sharpening steel that's been kept in your kitchen at home?" asked Hurlbut.

"Why'd I know that?"

"I don't know as you do. But we asked everybody else in the house and now I'm asking you."

"I don't know anything about it."

"Thank you. Now, Mrs. Ecke," he said, pulling the search warrant from his back pocket, "me and Carl are going to take a look around your barn. This paper says it's legal. When we get through, I'll come back and we'll talk some more. I'd appreciate it, Miz Ecke, if you don't leave for a while."

"I wasn't going anywhere."

"Fine." He turned to me. "Let's go."

It took a while but not as long as it might have, because Homer had shoved the sharpening steel into the hay in the farthest corner away from the haymow trapdoor, and that's where I looked first. It was against the wall and upright, where he'd stabbed it down.

We both looked it over carefully and couldn't be sure there was anything on it but a hint of rust near the guard.

"Okay," he said, "you were right about this. We'll go back and you ask the questions."

The session went on in the kitchen. We sat at the table with Hurlbut and me on one side facing Mae and Homer. Jennifer and Jack were at the table ends facing each other.

"I'm going to lay out the story," I said, keeping my eyes on Mae, "but before that we want you to know we think this was more than likely justifiable homicide. I'm telling you this so you'll see it's smart to fess up easy and save each other a lot of time and mess."

No one spoke. Mae kept looking me in the eye.

"Here are things we know. First, Basil threatened a while back to change his will if Jennifer didn't quit Jack. Basil told her to stay away from you because he figured you'd be encouraging her to move away from home. On the weekend before that Tuesday, he talked with old man Rutledge, the father of Jennifer's longtime friend, Colin, and learned Jennifer'd been in town with Jack, ignoring her promise to quit seeing him. On Tuesday night he found out from Terry that Jennifer was here. He jumped in his car and came storming out. He found Jennifer and Jack and he went nuts and attacked Mae. She grabbed the steel from the counter and let him have it. Everybody was scared to death when they figured he was dead and the first thing was to get him out of the house, so you piled the body into either Jack or Homer's car and brought it home. You found my car out on the blocks, one of you went in and talked with Terry, and hearing I'd had a run-in with Basil, tried to set me up."

All through this Mae's expression never changed, but she swallowed hard twice. I glanced at Jennifer, who was icy pale.

Homer kept his dumb look, and Jack smiled.

"That's a fine yarn you've spun," Jack said, "but you can't prove any of it. None of us saw any such thing or were involved in any way."

"If you all manage to stick with that, I'll admit it could get tough. But there's one little angle maybe you don't know. Some smart dude out east has come up with a way to test for blood on a thing like the steel we found hid in the loft. He can tell if it's human, and even if it's from a certain person. The steel will go to Aquatown and they'll work it over. Maybe they'll have to send it east. But sooner or later it'll do the trick. And then all four of you will be in the soup. They don't have to prove which one of you did it, they just got to prove it was done here and at that time. You all willing to go to jail?"

They avoided each other's eyes.

"It's lies," said Mae. "All that stuff about identifying blood. No jury'd believe such rot."

"They have and they will. Let me put it to you straight, Mrs. Ecke. I think you're the one who hit him. You've always hated him, you're a big, strong woman, and you were glad for an excuse to belt him and he gave it when he went at you."

"I didn't hit him until he knocked Homer down and started to kick him. He was aiming at his head and it was justifiable homicide and I'll admit it on one condition."

I looked at Hurlbut.

"What?" he asked.

"That it comes out there was nobody in this house but Homer and me. Otherwise I admit nothing and you can be damned."

Hurlbut's fat face almost turned long.

"I dunno—"

"Talk with the county attorney," I said. "Maybe it could get worked out. Especially if she confesses and claims either self-defense or justifiable homicide."

"All right," he said. "I'll talk to the attorney."

"No," said Mae. "It's between us in this room. Basil came out to threaten me, lost his temper, and attacked. Homer tried to defend me, Basil knocked him down and started kicking him, and I stopped him with the steel. Then we drove him home and left him in his yard. We didn't know he was dead, we thought he was just unconscious. Period. I did it, I'm sorry, but there was no choice, and it was unlucky all around I happened to hit him where it was fatal."

Everybody started talking then, but Mae waved them down and stuck with her position.

We left it there and drove back to town with the steel.

Of course, it wasn't as easy as all that. Once she got a lawyer he convinced her the blood tests wouldn't be accepted in a South Dakota court even if the process was possible. There was a lot of lawyer and prosecutor talk, and finally, to keep Jennifer from being involved in all the mess, Mae reaffirmed her confession. It was accepted by the DA and the case went to trial.

I drove Elaine to Minneapolis, and it was a nice trip maybe I'll report on another time. In case you're interested, no, she didn't put out. She'd promised her grandma, and Elaine was a girl who kept her word.

I looked up Evvie in Aquatown during a trip that way a year later and found her living in a fine small house in a good neighborhood. Jennifer, who'd married Jack and ran her father's drugstore, had given Evvie the shares Basil owned in the Bingham Hotel, and she was a partner-manager, getting along just dandy with Baxter, who was obviously nuts about her even though she kept him at a polite distance. I persuaded her to have lunch with me and asked, as it was nearing its end, what she'd done with the steel from her kitchen in Podunkville.

"I didn't do anything with it; Terry threw it in the river."

"Why?"

"Well, Terry got the whole story from Baxter, who listened in on talk between Jennifer and Jack the night it all happened. Mae had put our steel near Basil's body, but Terry thought that was more likely to involve him or me than you because nobody'd believe you'd been in our house. So he went out, found the steel, and threw it away."

I asked where Terry was now, and she said he'd been admitted to Princeton, thought he was in love with a girl from a neighboring college, and wrote to Evvie about every other month. I saw her several times after that and am happy to say she never made any restrictive promises to her grandma.